I0673206

In the Movies

The Richard Jackson Saga, Volume 4

Ed Nelson

Published by Ed Nelson, 2024.

Table of Contents

Other books by Ed Nelson

The Richard Jackson Saga

In the Richard Jackson World

Stand-Alone Story

Cast in Time Series

Dedication

This is dedicated to my wife Carol for her support and help as first reader and editor.

Also, the BHS class of 1962 just because.

Professionally edited by Janet E. Rupert

Quotation

That is exactly how it happened, give or take a lie or two.

James Garner as Wyatt Earp, describing the gunfight at the OK Corral in the movie *Sunset*.

Copyright © 2019

ISBN 979-8-89434-007-4
Library of Congress Control Number: 2022911369

Chapter 1

I was getting used to rising at four-thirty to exercise and run before going to the studio. At the studio, they first announced on Monday that we would take a one-week hiatus next week. We had been working long and hard, and it was time for a break.

When we came back, we would be doing our location shots. These would be out in Colorado at Mr. Easterly's ranch. This gave me a lot to look forward to. I would have to arrange a trip home and a side trip to Detroit to meet Mark Downing and tour Detroit Faucets.

The lead make-up artist asked me where she could get more of the hairdryers in makeup. They were working wonders for them. I told her they were doing the production tooling now and that the units would be available later.

"How much later?" she inquired.

"I would guess six months."

"Who should I make out the purchase order to? I need these now. The dryers will help with our shooting schedules tremendously."

After reflecting on getting thrown into a horse trough many times, I agreed with her and told her to make the order to Jackson Engineering.

While small for the studio, her purchase order was a lot to me. Ten thousand dollars would almost pay the startup costs.

The morning's shoot went well. I think everyone was energized by the idea of having a week off. While I was waiting for my next scene, the key grip from another set approached me.

"Rick, I'm John Dawson. We are having a problem setting up a shot over on sound Stage B. I've been told that you are good at mechanical things and maybe could help us."

We shook hands, and I told him, "No guarantees, but what is the problem?"

"We have to do a fight scene on top of a moving train. The director wants the fight to bounce around because of the track joints. This is before welded rail, so the joints really could bounce the car around."

I thought back to the clickity-clack I loved and remembered how we got tossed around inside the cars, so it must be a problem on top.

"I'm aware of that. What have you tried so far?"

"We tried bouncing the cameras, but that is what it looks like, the cameras moving, not the people. Our next step is to have stuntmen do the fight on top of a moving car with a camera suspended from the side of the boxcar."

"Even then, you would have to be moving at speed to get the effect the director wants. That is a recipe for disaster," I mused.

"You got it in one."

"So, modifying the cameras to bounce doesn't work. Using a real-life setup is too dangerous. That leaves a modified boxcar. How about cutting the top off a car and mounting it on something like walking beams or camshafts? That way, you could get the amplitude and frequency you need."

"Yeah, we could put airbags all around to reduce the falling danger. It would also allow us to set up several camera angles," the excited key grip added.

He continued, "It would be cheaper and easier to build a false boxcar top than to cut one off. Thanks, Rick, you have been a big help."

I'm unsure how much I helped, but it was a fun few minutes.

I saw Dick Wyman at lunch. He told me that he had used the hairdryer this morning after his shower, and he thought it was wonderful. While I was eating, my teachers Miss Sperry and Mr. Danson joined us and informed me that I had passed all my state exams, including Spanish, and had completed my freshman year. With Spanish, I had picked up an extra credit towards graduation. They wanted to know if I was ready to start the tenth grade.

"Wow, you guys know how to burst a bubble. I finish ninth grade today, and now you want me in tenth! Have you ever heard of summer vacation? On a more serious note, we only have three weeks to go. I haven't been asked to appear in anything else, so contacting Bellefontaine for my curriculum would probably be a waste of time."

"From a curriculum point of view, we would use the California schedule. Your studies would match the test. We were lucky this year, but I hate to count on it," Mr. Danson told me.

"Unfortunately, you are correct about not starting anything since you won't be here. It has been a pleasure; your results have made our company look good. You will be part of our presentation for our license renewal and work with other production companies."

"Do I get a fee?" I asked.

From the look on Miss Sperry's face, I had rained on her parade.

"I was only kidding. If it would help, I will give you a testimonial."

"That would be great!" enthused Mr. Danson.

I had redeemed myself with Miss Sperry. I hated to disappoint attractive women. She then let me know how pleased she was with her new hairdryer. Mr. Danson chimed in, "My wife is pleased. Also, she can get her hair wet while showering, and it still only takes fifteen minutes to be ready for work. She wants to know where she can buy them as gifts."

I had to inform them that they were six months or more from the marketplace.

After lunch, it was back to the set for more scenes. We spent till three o'clock doing walkthroughs for tomorrow's shooting. We had to be available for twelve hours a day. We rarely used all twelve hours. Since I was a child, the labor laws applied to me. The studio got around this by tracking the hours I worked. They didn't count the time I was waiting for other scenes. From what I was getting paid, I felt like I was the one doing the exploiting.

Even so, the state would check us out randomly to ensure I wasn't being worked to death. That in itself was a laugh. I was the fittest I had ever been in my life. The person who checked on us looked like he had been in Dachau. He looked so bad I felt sorry for him, though as Mum would say, he looked a decent chap.

He would check my hour log the studio was required to keep and ask me how things were going. He never gave anyone a hard time. I guess if guys like him weren't doing their job, there would be abuses like in the nineteenth century.

I went to the stunt area when the afternoon work was completed. I outfought Sammy with the real swords.

I got off to a fast start. With my rapier in sixte and posted, I performed a Balestra followed by a lunge and a counter beat, which disarmed him.

In English, I started with my sword blade straight out and pointing slightly up in the sixth position, which was the most basic dueling start. I held it in a post, meaning I had my fingers back a few inches on the hilt to give me more extension. This surrendered some strength and accuracy but was needed for what I was about to try. I had backed off about ten feet, which seemed like a lot but could be overcome quickly.

I took a forward leap, the Balestra, and then lunged at him. As I landed in position, I circled my sword under his and went up sharply, causing his sword to fly out of his hand. It was the first time I had ever had him at such a disadvantage. I think he was more excited than I was. I guess it validated his teaching.

Then he proceeded to thrash me soundly. Well, at least score more hits. He was still the teacher, and I was the student.

When it was time to lift, I was able to add more weight. I had to buy new shirts!

Chapter 2

Boxing was getting to be fun. Coach Palmer and I talked about what I was trying to achieve in my lessons. The one thing we both agreed on was that I wouldn't try to turn professional. From my point of view, there were two reasons. The first and main reason was self-defense. The second was to have the skill available if needed in a role. He thought those were very reasonable goals. He thought I had the basics down. What I needed now was a varied experience. This would involve me going up against various opponents of different skill levels.

He added one additional thought. "Boxing is a sport with rules. For self-defense, you need to fight with no rules."

"What would you suggest?"

"If you had the time, you could attend Ed Parker's Kenpo Karate School in Pasadena. The only problem is you would have to train almost every day for a year to become proficient. Your best bet is hiring an unarmed combat instructor who trained marines, not army."

"Why choose a marine trainer and not an army instructor?"

"Marines exist to fight. Semper Fi!"

There might be a bias at work here, but he was the coach.

"Do you know of anyone available?"

"Of course, I know someone, me! I'm a certified Black Belt trainer from my active-duty days."

So now, I have unarmed combat added to my training regime. His hourly rate was very reasonable.

He could get me to the Tan belt level with twenty-eight hours of training and another twenty-five hours to the Grey. This would make me proficient in basic techniques. Above that were the Green, Brown, and Black belts, but time would run out on the movie schedule before I could receive that training unless I wanted to stay in California and finish the levels.

I told him that I would be satisfied with the Tan and Grey belts for now. Not that I would get a belt, just the training. After the hiatus and location shoot, we agreed that I would box various opponents for two weeks. We would add an hour a day for unarmed combat during that time. When that was finished, we would train two hours a day. That way, I would be at the Tan level within five weeks. We would have to see what time, if any, remained to work on the Grey level.

Of course, it all depended on how quickly I could pick things up. My condition was better than most Marine recruits going into basic, so I had an advantage there. It would all depend on how fast I could master the techniques.

I stopped at the studio travel department and had them arrange my flight home on Saturday and return to Denver airport on Sunday week. On returning to my apartment, I made several calls. First, I called my reporter friends to check-in. None of them needed anything from me except a statement on Paul Grant.

We agreed that while I had professional disagreements with Paul Grant's behavior on the set, I was shocked and dismayed about his personal life. I was sorry that he was dead; I would not wish that on anyone, but at the same time, you sow what you reap. For each of the reporters, we came up with a slight twist of the words, so it didn't look like a planned statement but a frank interview.

The reporter for the *Los Angeles Examiner* told me that the gang wars had fizzled out and that the gangs were puzzled by what started it. Grant's death was the opening blow, but no one knew who had struck or why. Grant was considered a low-level dealer, selling to people on the sets, and no one was fighting for that territory. However, they had to react or appear weak once he was killed.

They were trying to figure out who had started it. Since no one was trying to replace him, the gangs were at a loss to explain how the conflicts started, so they just let it die out. It had been hard on the people caught in the middle but perceived as a cost of doing business.

Officially, the police were pleased with the cessation of violence. Unofficially, as one officer put it, "It's a shame all of the scum buckets didn't kill each other."

I called Anna Romanov. Her social secretary put me right through.

"Richard, I am so glad you called. I've outlined my goals with my new business. I'm going to take many different household products, have a design variation with my name, and sell them as the Romanov Collection."

She said this in a rush. You could hear the excitement.

"I'm going to Detroit Faucet this coming week if you could break free. You could spend some time with our designer."

"Can't the designer come to me?"

"Yes, she can, but think about this, you are about to put your name on a product manufactured by someone else. Won't you want to ensure that it is a real plant run by people who know what they are doing? You have to audition for parts. They should have to audition for you. The only difference is they can't bring their factory to you."

"Oh, I see what you mean. It could be fun. I have never been in a factory before."

I continued, "Are you available next Thursday? If you are, I would like to make an appointment for us, but let's make you a mystery guest. That way, there won't be any reporters there."

"I like that, Richard; this will be fun. I can fly in on Wednesday and stay at a hotel near the airport, and you can pick me up. Then I will fly home on Thursday night."

"Okay, let me make a phone call to make certain that Mark Downing, the majority owner, and our designer Sally Enright are both available. I'll call you right back."

I called Mark. He and Sally would be available. I did tell him that I might have a surprise guest. He wanted to know who it was, but I told him it wouldn't then be a surprise. After calling Anna back and giving her our home number in Bellefontaine so she could relay her travel arrangements, I called home.

Mum and Dad were thrilled with the idea of me coming home. They wanted to join the trip when I informed them of my Detroit plans. There was no reason they couldn't. We would also drive up on Wednesday evening, stay at the same hotel as Anna, and go to the plant as a group. They were pretty certain that Mrs. Hernandez would stay overnight with the kids.

Dad wanted to know if I had discussed any financial items with Miss Romanov. He was relieved when I told him no. He wanted to wait until we were in Detroit to have any serious discussions. He had no idea if she had realistic expectations.

Next on the agenda was the hairdryer. Dad had heard back from American Style. They would like to open discussions for an exclusive license. He asked me to get as much feedback as I could in writing. The actual order from the Warner Brothers makeup department would strengthen our hand.

He had sent off the gifts I had requested, including one each to Elizabeth and Ike. It seemed strange sending a hairdryer to a bald guy, but I didn't want him to feel left out if he learned I had sent one to the queen.

We tossed around ideas of what we should ask for but left it undecided.

We also discussed my buying a house here in California. We decided to put it on hold. I would be coming home in a month or so; the Paul Grant situation appeared to be settled, and I hadn't any movie offers to keep me here.

After that, Dad asked if I had planned a trip to Rowland Heights. I hadn't yet but improvised and told him that I was taking a trip down there after shooting tomorrow. Dad treated it with the respect it deserved, none.

"Please do it for me, Rick."

As we were about to hang up, Dad added, "Watch your mailbox. We have forwarded an interesting newspaper article to you." He wouldn't tell me anymore.

I called Nina. She updated me on her school day, boring, and then the social events of her day. It doesn't help when you don't know the players. I told her about my day and how I had started a self-defense class.

I told her about my trip home next week. I also let her know I was going to Detroit but didn't say anything about Miss Romanov joining my family. If nothing came of it, I didn't want to start any rumors. I had already seen how things got around in this town.

Overall, I don't think I missed school very much. I was working in an adult world. It was more interesting. Was I becoming an old man before my time? What nonsense. I'm only fifteen!

Later that night, I started a new thriller. The hero was sent to Crab Key to investigate the disappearance of a fellow operative, Commander Strangways.

Chapter 3

Tuesday started fine. After our morning rituals, Dick and I headed our separate ways to the studio. We pulled out of the apartment parking lot at the same time, and I tried to get him to drag, but he would have none of it. Just as well, I probably would've gotten a ticket.

At the studio's front gate, they told me Mr. Baxter would like to see me at the front office entrance. This was my agent, John Baxter. I wonder what he wanted to see me about. He had warned me that it could be as much as a year before I had another movie offer. If I didn't have one by a year, I probably wasn't going to get one.

He was all smiles, so I was correct in guessing it was good news.

"I've got an audition for you."

"What is it?" I inquired.

"It's a young Robin Hood type of adventure. The working title is *Bandits of Sherwood*. Since you are so good with a sword and bow, you will be a natural."

Now it was news to me that I was good with a bow. I hadn't handled one more than two or three times in my life, and they were more toys than the real thing. So, I did what they did in Hollywood, make-believe.

"I'm fairly good with a sword. I will have to work on the bow part."

"That's good. Your sword work will be much more important. They will do cutaways for any archery."

"When is my audition?"

"In about fifteen minutes. I checked with Ron Dodge, and he doesn't need you till after lunch, so you are good to go."

There is nothing like being thrown into the deep end.

"Where do we go, and am I dressed okay?"

"They don't care what you wear for this."

Mr. Baxter led me to another set where a director, Mr. Stanley Butler, was waiting with a small camera crew. He gave me some lines to read. I asked him if he wanted a British accent. He told me that it would be great if an American audience easily understood it. I switched to my Sir Nicklaus voice, and he loved it.

The producer was there though he sat there silently, and I wasn't introduced. I hadn't seen him around the lot, so I hadn't any idea who he was. He and Mr. Baxter were in a deep conversation while I worked on my audition lines.

I read through my lines silently a few times, then out loud. There were only a half dozen, so I memorized them on the spot. When I told them I was ready, they had me run through in front of the cameras without filming. Once they were satisfied with the lighting, we were ready to go. One nice thing I noticed was that the grips were people I had worked with before, and they seemed to be on my side. At least they took the time to get things correct.

I did two presentations for the camera, and Mr. Butler said that was enough. We had to wait several minutes for a stuntman to arrive. I was told the stuntman would be testing my ability with the sword. I strongly suspected who it would be. Sure enough, I heard Sammy as he was coming around the corner.

"These damn teenagers you bring in here have never held a sword and wouldn't know the pointy end if I stuck it in them."

About then, he caught sight of me. "Well, some of them know the pointy end. Hi, Rick."

He had brought protective gear for us with him but set all but the swords down. Let's do it, Rick. Show them what you have."

The director said, "Roll," Then we were at it. It was really fun. We were both showing off with different strokes and parries. We did some Errol Flynn stuff, jumping up on tables. All of a sudden, I heard, "Cut!"

"That was wonderful," exclaimed Mr. Butler. "Where did you learn that?"

I bowed as I pointed to Sammy, "My teacher, sir."

'We will call to let you know, but you are a strong contender for the part."

I heaved a sigh of relief. They hadn't asked me to draw a bow. I probably couldn't have drawn a real one with the biggest box of Crayola's.

As we were walking out, Mr. Baxter said, "You got the part."

"What do you mean? They said they will call, which means they want to see other people."

"That's what he said to save face. He could hear Tim Hughes and me talking. Tim knows all about your other movie with Wayne, and I told him about the TV special coming out in late spring. He also knows you have been on Jack Paar and regularly get into the entertainment columns."

"That makes you a draw. Butler also sees that the crew has picked you. They showed their support in the way they set you up. An upset crew can ruin a movie and, with it, a director's career. You have the part."

"Okay, what should I do now?"

"Try to use some of those magic contacts you seem to have in the press. That would force the issue if done properly. If they praise you as a pick for *Bandits of Sherwood,* it will be more pressure to select you. Now the question is how much you want to make on this movie. It is a B movie and will be doing good to gross ten million. That means you can make between one and three hundred thousand."

"Go for two hundred thousand and three points. The movie will have to break fifteen million for me to make three hundred thousand. That will show I have some skin in the game. Also, I would like to see an aggressive schedule like *Sir Nick,* starting on April 13 and finishing on May 18. That gives me one week off between pictures and then I can go back to Ohio for an event I have near the end of May."

"An aggressive schedule will keep the cost down. It will also have you working more than you have had to on *Sir Nick*."

"I know, but I have finished school for the year, so I have three to four hours more a day open."

"Are you some sort of genius who can learn quickly?"

"No, sir. I'm not dumb, but the important thing is that I'm organized and not afraid to work. Put that together with private tutoring so I can go through the material quickly. I've never had an I.Q. test, but I think I am normal or a little above, but nothing special."

"Well, Rick, you're accomplishing special things, so that makes you special in my book."

"Thank you, Mr. Baxter. Now I had better get over to my set."

"I will call as soon as I hear something."

"Okay."

I got to the set in time to see Mr. Wayne tear into a group of actors who hadn't done their homework. They played the role of the Regulators, the businessmen who had control of Johnson County. The three actors hadn't got their lines down pat and needed more run-throughs than necessary. I learned several new phrases. I didn't think you could do that sort of stuff with goats.

Rather than get involved with that mess, I went to lunch a half-hour early. Lunch was always fun; you would never know what you were going to see on any particular day. It looked like half the British Army from the Revolutionary War was there today, with Redcoats everywhere.

For some reason, there were always actors dressed as Indians. After a while, you didn't even notice them. To round it out, there were Spanish Conquistadors, 1920s Flapper Girls, two great white hunters, and of course, me, dressed as an 1890s cowboy. If you come back tomorrow, the costumes will change, but it will still have a wonderfully weird feel to it.

After lunch, till two o'clock, they had me in front of the camera. It was all talking in one setting rather than action shots, so it was just reciting lines. I was becoming fairly good at it, and my English accent was so ingrained that I had used it while shopping several times.

Today was different; I couldn't deliver a line correctly to save my life. I was so glad that Mr. Wayne had left the set. If he were present, he would be eating me alive. After an hour, the director threw up his hands in despair and told me to, "Get out of here, come back tomorrow ready to work!"

Chapter 4

Though it wasn't what I had planned, it worked in my favor as I was going to drive to Industry and go to the Workman–Temple residence. I had read up on the early history of California in the library. My ancestor's brother, John Rowland, had led a party of settlers, with William Workman, to be some of the first white American settlers in California.

They had settled in the LA area, both owning large tracts of land. The Rowland family, whom I had never met, still owned some of the original parcels in Industry. The Rowland house, which was the first brick structure in California, still stood. I would like to visit someday, but my mission was to check out Don Pio Pico's grave. He was the last Mexican governor of California.

His remains were moved to the Workman-Temple family graveyard in 1921. I was hoping that whatever I was looking for was buried behind his tombstone. I had cut up a coat hanger to make a probe. If it was buried deeper than that, I wasn't going to find it. I'm not about to go digging big holes in a graveyard. It just wouldn't be right. Besides, it would scare the heck out of me if I hit a coffin.

The drive down was pleasant. I had to stop for gas once. The gas cap located behind the license plate was convenient. I wondered how it would work with a continental kit. I had thought about having one added but decided not to.

Getting back on the road, I came up behind a gasoline tanker. I had to back off a long way. The chains at the back of the tanker to ground it from static electricity were kicking stones on the road up. I finally gave up, pulled over, and got an ice cream cone from a Tastee-Freez. That let the truck move farther away. The ice cream was good also.

I arrived at the Workman-Temple house to find an abandoned, overgrown mess. The house was in great disrepair. It would take a major effort to restore it. Since no one was around, I walked around the back of the house and found the family graveyard. It didn't take much hunting to find the graves of Don Pio Pico and his wife.

I returned to my car and retrieved my coat hanger probe. I took a long look around, but no one was in sight. Returning to the grave, I probed behind the back of the tombstone. About two feet out, I hit resistance about six inches in the ground. Probing around, it appeared to be a rectangle of four inches by twelve inches.

I returned to my car and drove into Industry, stopping at a hardware store to buy a garden trowel. I headed back to the cemetery, where there still was no one in sight. I dug up the combination of sod and desert sand around the spot I had probed and set it aside. I then dug down deeper to find a metal box wrapped in an oilcloth.

The box was not locked. Upon opening it, I found a handwritten note.

"If you find this note, please call this telephone number and state you're calling on the lost family. After writing down the phone number, please rebury the note in the box."

William Rowland signed it.

I wrote down the number on the back of my ever-present little black book. Everyone carried one to write down phone numbers. Of course, if you were a teenage boy, they were supposed to be girlfriends. I didn't have very many numbers, and most of them were adults like Scout leaders, Jackson Engineering contacts, guys at school, or movie business contacts.

What did that say about me? The only girls I had numbers for were Janet Huber, Pam Schaffer, Judy King, Cheryl Hawthorne, and now Nina Monroe. Not an impressive score, according to all the songs I heard.

After that, I reburied the box, wondering what it was all about. I headed back home. This was Dad's to sort out. It was past ten o'clock in Ohio when I got home, so I didn't call. What I did was practice my lines. Knowing them hadn't been the problem. It was saying them with the proper conviction.

I was used to succeeding in most things I tried. I didn't like today's failure at all. I had managed to put it aside when I went down to Industry, but now was the time to face it. When I went over my lines, they didn't feel right to me. I pulled the original script and reread it instead of using the daily shooting script.

When I reread it, it dawned on me. There was a problem, and I was it. I was taking the scene out of context. Movies were never shot as a straight-through story but as the logistics and economics dictated. Sir Nick's character had been growing as the story went along, starting as your basic upper-class spoiled brat to a capable young man who takes responsibility for his actions.

This scene was a throwback to his development. I was trying to play it as responsible Sir Nick instead of spoiled Sir Nick. It wasn't the words I was saying. It was the body language I was using. Using this discovery, I went over the lines again, and they fell into place.

Wednesday morning, I couldn't rush through my daily routine fast enough. Dick Wyman had to get me to slow down on the track. He wanted to know where the fire was. I explained how I had screwed up yesterday and now had a chance to redeem myself.

He told me not to make too big of a deal about it. All actors went through it several times in their careers. They would forget where the scene fits into the movie and do it all wrong. The trick was to figure out the problem, apologize, do it right, and move on. The worst thing I could do was blame other people for my problems.

Since I knew I was the problem, why would I want to blame someone else? If I had a motto, it would be, fix it and move on.

At the studio, my first act arriving at the set was to find Ron Dodge and apologize for yesterday's performance. He agreed with my take on the problem and told me it was okay, but I had to get it right today.

Fortunately, I did. It didn't seem natural to me to be a spoiled brat, but I channeled Paul Grant, and it worked. One thing I thought of last night. I had always accused Denny and Eddie of being spoiled brats. I now understood they were anything but. The one in danger of being spoiled was Mary. She had three brothers who doted on her.

Eddie, who was closer to her in age, didn't put up with as much nonsense as Denny and me. Even as I thought about that, I realized we didn't let her get away with things completely, like cheating at Monopoly. The more I thought about it. She wasn't that spoiled, either.

Paul Grant would be my role model for spoiled from now on. I had the gross thought that he had been dead long enough that his corpse would be spoiling by now. Yuck!

Ron Dodge came over to me as we finished shooting before lunch. "Rick, you are turning into a professional actor. You had a bad day like everyone has and bounced back. You handled it maturely, not taking out your shortcomings on the rest of the world. That is rarer than you may think. You seem like an adult in a child's body."

"Thank you for your kind words. May I ask a favor?"

"Within reason," he replied.

"Could you have a daily script written up where I get to throw Mr. Wayne in the water trough?"

"Are you serious?"

"Just as a joke; it would be great to see the look on his face."

He chuckled as he replied, "Strike that comment about being an adult in a child's body."

Lunch was the usual parade of people dressed from across the world and the ages. I was joined by the key grip who had asked me about the boxcar.

"It worked well. We rigged up a set to give the motion. It worked so well, that we are now having the box car top being built. There is no doubt it will work. I will be the key grip on the *Bandits of Sherwood*. I'm looking forward to working with you."

"You know more than I do. No one has called me yet."

"They will soon. Your agent is in negotiations as we speak. From what I hear, you will like the deal."

It is a small tight world we live in, and there aren't any secrets. I should remember that.

After lunch, it was back to the salt mines, well, the movie set. Mr. Wayne was there, all dressed and ready to go. One of the writers came around and handed us all a new daily script. I suspected its contents and jumped down to the end.

I got there just as an explosive yell came out from Mr. Wayne.

"There is no way in hell he is going to throw me in a horse trough!"

We all burst out laughing, led by Mr. Dodge. Mr. Wayne caught on immediately.

"Who put you up to this, Ron?"

Mr. Dodge was still laughing but managed to point toward me. I would've thought he would have waited at least a minute before throwing me to the wolves.

Mr. Wayne shook his fist at me and said, "You will pay, Ricky, when you are least expecting it."

Now that was a threat to fear from someone with Mr. Wayne's resources. We settled down and were able to get two scenes in the can. While I wasn't invited to see the overnight rushes, I had been told that things were going well.

After we were done at five o'clock, I went to the stunt area for my workout.

Chapter 5

After my lifting, I hunted Sammy up for swordwork.

Sammy had another man with him, Rod Bell. Rod was an archer. They didn't even have to tell me. All the gear he had told the story for him.

After introductions, I was given a tour of the bow. It was a full-size six-and-a-half-foot English longbow. Rod had me try to draw it. I was able to pull it back easily. I commented on this, and he laughed.

"This is a beginner's training bow; it has a twenty-five-pound draw. If you couldn't pull that, we would be taking you to the doctor. A regular longbow used in war could have a draw of over one hundred and fifty pounds. Today a sixty-pound pull is the norm."

"We will work you up to a sixty-pound bow. That will force you to go through the proper motion to draw a bow. This will look good on the screen."

"What is the proper motion? I thought you held your left arm stiff and pulled the string back with your right arm."

"Not at all. You keep the string in your right hand up tight to your anchor point and bend your whole-body weight into the horn of the bow to draw it."

He demonstrated it to me and had me practice the motion. My anchor point was my chin, where the string touched my body when the bow was fully drawn.

"Also, we have to fit you with a bracer so that you won't tear your arm or hands apart. You are big enough to use standard, three-foot-long arrows."

"Rick, it takes a lot of practice to become accurate with a bow, more than a handgun. We don't have time for that. A trained archer will do any shots in the film. We will show you drawing the bow correctly and loosing, but that won't be the arrow flight shown."

I knew I wasn't an archer, but this burst my bubble. We worked for half an hour on the proper drawing of a bow. Rod told me he would bring a bow with a forty-five-pound pull tomorrow to see how I did with that. The higher the poundage I could pull, the more realistic it would look on the screen.

I hadn't said anything, going with the flow, but everyone seemed to think I had this movie part.

We skipped swordwork, and Sammy thought I was more than capable of doing any of the choreographed fights for the movie. That's right, choreographed, just like a dance. Nothing was left to chance. That way, each fight would come out as they wanted it.

I could take him down immediately if it were a minor bad guy. The climax fight with the major baddie would require him to get the upper hand and for me to fight back.

At boxing, it was a bag and footwork only. It took an hour but seemed much shorter. I certainly needed a shower. At my apartment door, there was a package. When I opened it, there was the cigar box I had requested and another unopened package.

The unopened package was posted from the Shawnee Nation. When I opened it, there was an article from the tribal paper and a presentation box. I opened the presentation box first. It was a silver medal similar to the one that was given to Chief Blackhoof, but instead of the president's profile, it had Blackhoof's profile. It also had a small number 001 on it. The medal was suspended from a leather cord so it could be worn around the neck.

The box itself had an engraved plate with the message, "Richard Jackson, a friend of the Shawnee, 1959."

Wow!

After I calmed down and had examined and admired the medal enough, I read the article. It told how the Blackhoof collection of medals was found in the tribal archives based on information provided by Richard Jackson. This rare collection was the most complete of all the presentation medals ever found and would be on display in the Shawnee Historical Museum.

Mr. Jackson has been presented with medal number one of the newly founded Blackhoof medal to be presented to those who have proven themselves to be a true friend of the Shawnee as long as the sun rises. I wonder if they will ever give one to a politician.

I called Bellefontaine and talked to the family. I told Dad about my adventure at the Workman-Temple residence. It was now a rundown house. I told him of my find and gave him the phone number and the phrase to use. He told me he would try it, he hadn't any hopes of there being anything of value, but this could be interesting.

I told him about the Blackhoof medal, and he laughed.

"You will get a kick out of this. The Logan County Historical Society was setting up the Manary Blockhouse, and the workers found the hidden compartment. There have been all sorts of guesses about what may have been stored there. None of them have been close."

Dad also had some additional family news. His two half-brothers in Indiana tried to make up for their lack of funds by running moonshine. They were now facing five years in the penitentiary. Their mother had called trying to raise money for a lawyer, but Dad declined.

I spent some time with my brothers and sister even though I would be home on Saturday. Last night's thoughts had made me realize how much I missed them. Mary wanted to know if I had been to Disney yet.

She just said, "Oh." When I told her, "No?"

But I could tell she was disappointed.

Next, I followed my agent's advice and called my media contacts. They were all interested in the new movie and me having a role. The

LA paper person had already heard and was planning a piece. As usual, I gave each a separate quote.

As an extra tidbit, I talked about John Wayne and the fake script, where I got to throw him in the horse trough. I figured he was going to get me, so I should take it as far as I could. They couldn't wait to hear what his revenge would be. This was appreciated as inside news and helped cement my relations. Maybe I did have magic contacts, as Mr. Baxter called them.

Last I called Nina and asked her what she was doing on Friday.

There was going to be a small dinner party at her house. Would I be her plus one?

"What is a plus one?"

She explained that rather than "and guest," the term was "plus one."

The rich even talk differently.

I told her I had a small gift for her dad. Of course, she had to know what it was. She was amazed when I told her about the unopened box of cigars.

"Ricky, the open box with two cigars is my dad's pride and joy. This will blow him away. Where did you find it, and how can you afford to give it away so casually?"

I explained that I had found it. As far as its value, it had cost me nothing and was sitting in a closet. Why shouldn't I give it to someone who collects them?"

"Still, it is a very generous gift. He will want desperately to do something for you."

"The only things I could use right now are gifts for my brothers and sister from Disneyland."

"I think we may have items that would work. What are their ages again?" she asked me. She then confirmed the dress code for Friday. It was what I thought of as California casual, slacks, a golf shirt, and a jacket.

My last call was to Mark Downing. Now that it was confirmed, I figured I had better tell him about Anna Romanov. He about flipped when I told him she wanted to have her name on some of the designer faucets in our line. The fact that she would be in his factory next Thursday shook him up. When I hung up, I figured he was about to lose a week's production as the plant was cleaned. That might not be a bad thing.

I watched an episode of *Mr. Ed* and then went to bed. I read a detective story set in Esmeralda, California. I would have to look that up as I had never heard of it. It had it all: murder, blackmail, revenge. I think the line I liked best in the whole story was "There was nothing to it. The Super Chief was on time, as it almost always is, and the subject was as easy to spot as a kangaroo in a dinner jacket."

Chapter 6

Thursday was another day. Up early, exercise, run, have a quick breakfast at the studio commissary, and work on the set. Notice I said work on the set. I don't know when acting became a job to me, but it did. It was a good enjoyable job, but it didn't feel like I was getting a day off from school anymore.

Would I want this job forever? No, but I had no idea what I wanted to do. It would have something to do with humans in space, but what? It wouldn't be as an astronaut. I was too tall. The height limit was six foot three inches. I'm six-four. It would be as a passenger at a much later date.

The more likely possibility was that I would drive projects that would help explore space. That would take money, lots of money. Well, I was working on that. Unfortunately, it was a lot of money on a personal basis, not a corporate basis. What I was thinking of would take Lockheed or Boeing sort of money. Well, that was a project for a later date.

As a team, we were able to get through several scenes today. I appeared to be over my acting problems. I was okay if I reread the script to know where Sir Nick was on his growth curve. I wish it were this easy in real life. He always progressed forward. My life seemed to go two steps forward and one back.

It made the day more interesting when I heard a voice behind me say, "Partner, when you least expect it."

Time goes fast when you are looking over your shoulder continuously. I thought I'd had it at lunch when someone popped a paper bag behind me. It seems the whole studio knew about Mr. Wayne's promise and was trying to "help" out.

After lunch, it was back to work until six o'clock. I did my lifting at the stunt area, but everyone else had left, so I headed home. I stopped at a Burger Chef and then went back to the apartment. I unlocked the door to a ringing telephone. It was the reporter from the LA paper.

He wanted to know how I had gotten such a good deal for appearing in *Bandits of Sherwood.* I told him I hadn't been told I had the part, much less what the deal was. He had a hard time believing me. It was all over the street. He hung up, disappointed that I couldn't tell him any more, but I think he believed me.

I had barely hung up when the phone rang again. It was Mr. Baxter. I couldn't help it. "I hear I got a really good deal on the part."

"Where did you hear that?"

"The *LA Examiner* just hung up."

"It is impossible to keep a secret out here. Yes, you got a wonderful deal, two hundred and fifty thousand and four points."

"Really!" I didn't squeal. Girls squeal.

I just made several high-pitched yells.

"Really," he replied. "Please tone it down. You are going to ruin my hearing."

I managed to quiet down.

"That is great, Mr. Baxter. What about the shooting schedule?"

"That is why you got so much; they are anxious to get this film done. It is being squeezed in before another commitment, so they were thrilled that you wanted an aggressive schedule."

"Mr. Baxter, I appreciate all your efforts on my behalf."

"Rick, it has been my pleasure. Becoming your agent may have saved my life, and I know it saved my granddaughter. You are our hero."

"I'm glad I could help."

"I would like to have a serious discussion with you as to where you want to take your career."

"Can it wait till after I get back? We are on hiatus next week, then on location in Colorado."

"There is no hurry. I just would like to get a feel for your goals in life, so I know what parts to go after."

"Fair enough, but I must warn you that I may not want to make my mark in life by being in the movies."

"That is what I have to know. Let's talk about it later. May I also suggest calling the LA paper back and giving them an update? You need them on your side."

"I will do that and talk to you later."

"Good night, Rick."

I called the LA reporter back and updated him on my conversation. I told him the details of the deal and that they went for it because I was willing to work an aggressive schedule.

I may have been a little misleading. I left him with the idea that my work ethic made me attractive to them rather than the fact that I had requested the schedule. I wanted to attend the Scout camporee and go on my summer vacation.

I spent some time selecting the clothes I would take to Ohio. I had bought new clothes that fit better since I had started lifting weights. I was glad that I broke down and bought a new suit. It was a dark blue with very thin muted red pinstripes. It was the first suit that I had tailored, so it had my name embroidered on an inside pocket.

I read an adventure story for the rest of the evening. It was during World War II, set in the Aegean Sea. Coastal guns were blocking a strait the British needed to pass through to rescue some prisoners. Commandos led by the Human Fly, Keith Mallory from New Zealand, climbed the cliffs and destroyed the guns. I felt sorry for Lt. Stevens and thought Panayi got his just desserts.

Friday was a hard day for everyone. We all wanted to start our hiatus. Even Mr. Wayne had a hard time concentrating on his lines. At lunchtime, Mr. Dodge gave up.

"Get out of here, you bums. I'll see those scheduled at the Easterly Ranch a week from Monday. If you don't have directions to the ranch yet, be sure to get them before you leave."

Everyone scattered. I had lunch in the commissary. After that, I wandered over to the stunt area. Rod Bell, the archery instructor, was over at the butts. He had some time, so he agreed to fit my armguard and let me shoot some arrows.

First, he established that my right eye was my dominant eye and that I was right-handed. That simplified things as I could use a right-hand bow.

The armguard was like they would have used in medieval times. It wrapped around my whole arm and part of my hand, acting as a finger tab to protect it while I drew and loosed an arrow. He had several sizes to choose from, so I had a good fit.

Again, he taught me to have my forward foot standing in line towards the target. Then place the arrow on the arrow rest, and then nock the arrow, hold the string to an anchor point with three fingers. For me, the anchor point was my chin. Next, push the bow out and bring the arrow up to the target.

It proved easiest if I bent forward a little and pushed the bow away as I straightened up, putting my back into the push. I could see that after practice, I would end up on my aim point in one smooth motion.

I went through the motion several times. Mr. Ball was pleased.

"That is a sixty-pound bow. When drawing it, your motions and body strain are exactly what they would be if shooting a one-hundred-and-fifty-pound draw bow. The only difference is about twenty years of practice to build strength."

I'm a golfer, but I am not an archer. I could hit the target most of the time, but not once did I get the bull's eye. The truth be told, I didn't get any in the second ring, either. Mr. Ball told me I had done quite well for a beginner. The important thing—I had the style and could shoot an arrow in the movie.

They would cut away from me while a real archer made the shot. Since it was a movie, the archer may not make the shot on the same day or even in the same state. That was all good, but it didn't help my ego. I was so used to being able to do everything that it was a little hard to accept that I wasn't a natural archer.

Mr. Ball must have sensed that because he told me that no one had ever picked up the bow and was immediately an expert. It took years to train an archer for the military. It sounded good but didn't make me feel better. I tried hard not to come off as pouting.

I did my lifting, after which I went to the gym to see if I could box. No one was there, so I hit the bags a little but couldn't get into it, so I headed home.

It was the first week of March, and the weather was getting nicer, but no one was in the pool yet. I sat out and read some more in a book from the library about the economics of running a business. There was a lot I needed to learn. I could see that there were many university courses in business in my future if I followed my apparent path.

As I closed the book, I realized that it was a library book, and it and the others in the apartment would be overdue by the time I got back, so I grabbed them all and drove to the library. The library was on the corner of two busy streets. As I was walking out of the parking lot, an elderly lady with a two-wheeled pull cart full of groceries was getting ready to cross the street.

She would never get across the way she moved before the light changed, so I offered to help her. She took me up on my offer. When I got her to the other side, she told me, "You know you look a lot like that horrid Rick Jackson."

"Oh, why is Rick Jackson horrid?" I inquired.

"He said all those awful things about my Paul Grant before he was murdered."

"You are related to Paul Grant?"

"Oh no, I just loved his TV show."

"Well, you have a nice day, ma'am."

What can I say?

From the library, I went home, showered, and put on fresh clothes for the dinner party at Monroe's. I was at their door at the appointed time. I had my present for Mr. Monroe in a paper bag. I didn't have the time or inclination to wrap it. More like the inclination, but I don't think Mr. Monroe would care.

He didn't. His eyes got big when he pulled the cigar box out of the bag.

"Rick, where did you find this?"

I shared the whole story with him.

"Do you realize that this could go for twenty thousand dollars at an auction?"

"Nina told me it was valuable, but you heard how it has been sitting in my closet. My parents didn't think it was a big deal to give it to someone who would appreciate it."

"Did they realize how much it is worth?"

"We never discussed it, but we aren't hard up by any means. Please just accept the gift in the spirit it is given."

"Okay, Rick, but I owe you one. I can't wait to show this to Darryl Zanuck. He will eat his heart out."

Nina broke in, "Daddy. I'm making a small down payment on your debt. Rick will be in trouble with his brothers and sister if he doesn't bring them something from Disneyland. I took the liberty of using your Rolodex and made a phone call to your contact at Disney. He messengered up some items."

She gave me three wrapped gifts, in Disney paper, of course. They were labeled for Denny, Eddie, and Mary.

Using their ages to choose the gifts, Mr. Dixon sent up a Mickey Mouse watch for Eddie, a tie for Denny with small pictures of Mickey, and for Mary a complete princess outfit, including a tiara.

I forgot myself and kissed her right in front of her father. He took it in good stride and told me not to expect a kiss from him for the cigar box! I don't know which flustered me more, kissing Nina in front of her dad or her dad talking about kissing me.

The other dinner guests began arriving. Among them were Mr. George Burns, along with Gracie Allen, who had just retired from show business. Milton Berle was there with I think it was his third wife, but I wasn't sure. Mr. Burns and Mr. Berle are cigar smokers, so Mr. Monroe was eager to share his new display piece. Mr. Berle offered him thirty thousand dollars on the spot, but it was declined. If it had been me, I might have taken it.

The dinner conversation was interesting, with tales of the early days. Nina and I listened without trying to add to this conversation. The adage that children should be seen and not heard came to mind.

After dinner, Nina and I took a walk out to the pool house and necked for a while. After half an hour, we heard a door open and a cough, so we took the hint and said good night. I had to get up early for my flight, so it was time for me to leave.

Chapter 7

My flight was early Saturday, so I skipped my running and was ready when the hired car pulled into the drive. I had decided that I didn't want to leave the T-Bird at LAX for the two weeks I would be on hiatus and at the Easterly Ranch, so I asked the studio to call a car for me this morning. Of course, being Hollywood, it was a full-stretch limo.

At the airport, the check-in went easy. Having a driver take care of your luggage curbside and then having an airline representative escort you to the Ambassador Club, with your ticket and boarding pass waiting for you, really helped. I could get used to this level of service.

There was the obligatory photo op as I boarded the plane. After I got settled into first class, people started approaching me for my autograph. A stewardess asked several people to wait till we were in the air to ask me, as it was delaying boarding. No one asked what I thought of all this, but I did the graceful thing and signed away.

The flight was long and boring. No one was sitting beside me so I was able to read during the whole trip in peace. I was still struggling with the finances of a business. It looked like a lot of work and opportunity at the same time.

By the time I got to Dayton, I was ready for bed. The studio had even arranged for a ride from Dayton to Bellefontaine, though it was only a regular car, a Lincoln, but not a limo. How soon we are spoiled!

Everyone was up and excited when I got home. My gifts, or more rightly Nina's, were a hit. I confessed how they were obtained; the kids didn't care, but Mum and Dad wanted to know a lot more about Nina.

I told them I was very tired, which was true, putting off the inquisition until tomorrow. One thing had changed, my room was now Mary's, and I had hers. I knew it was coming, but it was still a bit of a shock. It didn't keep me awake at all.

Sunday was wonderful. We had a nice family breakfast. I got caught up in all the gossip. Tom and Tracey had broken up. I guess it was considered a week-long tragedy at school. I would have to remember that if I ran into either of them this week.

I did explain my relationship with Nina, just friends working on boy/girlfriend status. I may have dodged the truth on that, but I didn't want to worry my parents about what may be going on in California, or in this case, not going on. How do you say to your parents "I'm not sleeping with that girl."?

I wimped out and downplayed things. Besides, Nina and I had sort of drifted together. We had made no announcements. It just sort of happened.

We talked about American Style, a beauty products company. They had come up with the million dollars and agreed to five percent of the selling price on each hairdryer unit for an exclusive license. So now I was a millionaire. I still couldn't open a checking account.

Dad updated me on Jackson Housing. The company now owned fifty-two units in five cities. This would give Mum and Dad around a hundred thousand dollars a year in their name. Our family was doing well.

I was surprised about how mature Denny was getting. He acted like a real person. Eddie and Mary were still little kids. I didn't realize how much I was missing them until I got home. We spent the afternoon doing important things like reviewing our NCAA basketball tournament brackets. I was out of it as I hadn't read sports magazines while in California.

I favored California to win the championship even though West Virginia had Jerry West playing for them. I didn't even know who played for California, but I felt I had to support them because I was now living there.

We also talked about Wednesday's trip to Detroit for the plant tour on Thursday. Mum and Dad wanted to know about Anna Romanov and how I met her. This led to long stories about the dinner party at Monroe's and all the guests. Denny was about freaked when he heard I had introduced Paul Anka to Annette. In the teen's circles, it was considered the biggest thing since Romeo and Juliet.

That is how Sunday went. It was wonderful to be at home.

Chapter 8

It was strange waking up at my real home on Monday morning. To add to that, I had nothing to do, well, almost nothing. The point is I didn't have to jump out of bed and start moving immediately. I luxuriated for ten minutes but had to get up for the obvious reason. I had to pee.

That started my day. After my morning pushups and sit-ups, I dressed for running. March had come in like a lion in Ohio, but today was mild. I put my five miles in on my old route up around the airbase and back. Nothing had changed. I only was gone for five weeks. It seemed like forever.

In the five weeks, I had completed ninth grade, started learning how to box, studied sword fighting, attempted surfing and archery, and took up weightlifting. It may be bragging, but I was on my way to becoming a professional actor. If not, I sure had some people fooled.

I was now a millionaire, not on paper, real money. The American-style deal, which was for an exclusive license, had put me over the top. I hadn't kept close track, but I was halfway there before this deal. With the percentage on each sale of an adjustable showerhead, I would be a millionaire by the end of the year. The money from my movie work was significant in its own right.

By any standard, I was now rich. Why didn't I feel any change? Maybe I would feel different after my first ten million or a hundred million. I think a billion came next, but I had to check. By the time I got to this level of stupid thinking, I had completed my run.

There was an interesting statement last night from my dad. "I have so much happening this week. You will have to arrange your transportation."

When I returned home, the family was sitting down for breakfast. Even Mary was up and being her grumpy morning self.

Her grumpiness was offset a little by her princess outfit. It is hard for a five-year-old to be grumpy when she is wearing a tiara. We would ignore her until after she had her cereal and watched cartoons for a while.

Everyone else was wide awake. Denny was ready for school. He had on slacks, a blue shirt with a button-down collar, a dark blue sports coat, and a Mickey Mouse tie. He looked very preppy.

I told him so, and he smiled and responded, "The girls like the look!"

"I bet they do; have some fun little brother."

Eddie had to show me he was wearing his watch, so all my gifts had been a hit. Mum was listening to this exchange. I should have known she was paying attention for a reason.

"Last night, you told us that a girl named Nina arranged for the gifts."

It was easier to tell her about how I had met her and that we had several dates, but there was nothing serious.

"What do you mean by serious, Rick?"

"We haven't said we are exclusive and only kissed several times."

"Where does she live?"

I swear she was trained as a professional interrogator. If I didn't answer all this, there would be bright lights and rubber hoses. Not really, but Mum didn't give up once she got going.

That worked out because it gave me the opening to talk about Mr. Monroe and his position at Warner Brothers, his house, the parties, and the people I had met. Again, Denny was amazed by my introduction to Annette and Paul Anka. He told me I was stupid. I should have kept her for myself.

Before I could give a reply, which would get me into trouble, Dad looked at his watch and told the boys it was time for them to leave for school.

After they left, my parents and I chatted more casually over coffee. Dad gave me a detailed update on Jackson Housing. There were now five offices, ones in Bellefontaine, Kenton, Urbana, Saint Mary's, and Wapakoneta. Each office had a rent manager and two handymen for the upkeep of the apartments.

Dad had arrangements with real estate brokers in each town to scout properties out for him. He even had to expand the office in Bellefontaine as a headquarters. He rented the floor above as his business office. The staff was comprised of a bookkeeper and a secretary. He was considering adding a purchasing agent to make deals with the local supply houses as the company was buying many materials to update the houses.

He was now thinking of further expansion beyond these cities. It looked like my dad was going to end up a millionaire in his own right. That did give me pause for thought.

"Mum and Dad, the company is set up that I will inherit it because it was my seed money that started it. I've enough money that I would never have to work again in my life. I think you should restructure the company so that the other kids have an interest."

Mum and Dad glanced at each other.

"Rick, you must have read our minds. We were going to offer you a buyout or some sort of deal so that we could do exactly that."

"That's settled. Just include us all equally, and it's done."

"I'll do that, Rick. At the same time, Eugene Burke has recommended that we make Jackson Housing a holding company and have each office in the various cities be a separate company. That way, if there is a problem in one area, we aren't ruined completely."

"That makes sense. I should do that with the showerhead, my acting career, and the hairdryer. Have Richard Jackson Enterprises own three separate companies. I think I will talk to Mr. Burke about that while I'm downtown.

"That brings up another issue, transportation. Unless you have objections, I would like to buy a car for use in Bellefontaine. Mum could use it when I'm not here."

"What are you thinking of, Rick?" asked Mum.

"I would like another T-Bird. I love that car."

Dad laughed and held out his hand to Mum, "You owe me a dollar."

She got her purse and grudgingly paid Dad. "I felt sure you would ask for a Corvette."

"It's a nice car, Mum, but I just love the T-Bird for some reason."

"Rick, it's your money, and you have a lot of it. Why not enjoy it? That does bring up a more serious question.

"Where should your money be? Right now, it is in the bank, drawing a little interest. It should be invested in something more profitable."

"I've no idea how to do that."

"I don't either. We have to see Eugene Burke. I'll call him to see when he is available, and maybe he can help us."

Dad made the phone call and was lucky enough to catch Mr. Burke as he opened his office for the week. He told Dad that he would have time this morning if we could come down right away. After that, he was tied up for the week.

I did have time for a quick shower. As we were leaving, I told Mum that my hair was dry, so "I won't catch my death."

She muttered something about, "Maybe I did the wrong one." Whatever she meant by that.

At the attorney's office, Mr. Burke explained what had to be done to separate my businesses. He thought it an excellent idea for two reasons. The first was that it would protect my business ventures from each other.

He stopped, so I had to ask, "What is the second reason?"

"I'll get to charge you a lot of money for doing it."

After I was done groaning, he explained what it would cost. It wasn't that much. There would be Jackson Productions, Jackson Home Products, and Jackson Personal Products, all wholly-owned subsidiaries of Jackson Enterprises. For a mere fifteen hundred dollars, he would handle everything. That wasn't a bad deal for all the filings he would have to do with the state and county.

He even went further and explained that Jackson Enterprises would be set up as a State of Delaware registered company for tax purposes. He asked me who my accountant was. I looked at Dad desperately. It was like the ground had opened up under me. I was lost.

"I don't have one."

"Rick, you should hire a firm as quickly as you can. Your cash flow must be enormous. If you don't get an accounting firm busy, you will owe more taxes than you can believe. You need to be able to write off all your California expenses. I know you hired engineering help with your hairdryer project. That can all be written off."

"Who would you suggest?"

"Locally, Grimes Accounting is considered the best. Both father and son are CPAs. If you want, I can call Robert Sr. and see if he or Jr. has time for you today."

"That would be appreciated, but before you call, is there a stockbroker in town who you recommend?" asked Dad.

"There is no question there. The national firm, James Daniels, was founded right here in Bellefontaine. Their local manager is Bill Schwab."

Both Dad and I told Mr. Burke that we wanted to proceed with the companies, the accountants, and the broker. When I woke up this morning, I had nothing to do!

Mr. Burke made the calls and told us we were welcome anytime this morning. We thanked him for all his help and made our way to the accounting firm. Robert Jr. was available. Robert Jr. must have been sixty. I would like to meet Robert Sr. During our talks, Robert the Third sat in while we were served coffee by the Third's daughter Roberta. Talk about your family business!

Roberta was pretty, but she was also about twenty-five years old. Dad and I both explained our needs. Robert Jr. laughed and asked us when we could bring our shoeboxes full of receipts. Dad took a little umbrage at that. His bookkeeper kept good files in his office.

After Junior made peace with Dad, I told him, "I will have to buy a pair of shoes."

"Why is that?"

"So, I will have a shoebox to keep my receipts in. Right now, they are lying on my desk in my apartment."

"Just bring them down later today, and we will start sorting them out."

"Uh, my apartment is in Burbank, California."

"I thought so," broke in Roberta. "Grandpa. This is the actor Ricky Jackson."

"Humph, I haven't seen any of your work."

"Sir, I'm not surprised. My first movie with John Wayne will be released this summer."

That changed everything. I dropped the right name. Mr. Wayne was a hero to the entire Grimes family. Dad and I described how our businesses were going to be set up. Notes were taken like crazy. We both permitted them to contact Mr. Burke and let him know he would share our company's information as they were established.

Suddenly, it was lunchtime! The morning passed quickly. Dad and I went to Isley's for a quick sandwich. At one o'clock, we were at the brokers.

After going over all the options, it looked like I would be a stockholder in what they called blue-chip companies, such as Coca-Cola and IBM. There would also be some long-term U.S.

Treasuries in my portfolio. Who would have thought I would have a portfolio when I woke up this morning?

I would keep ten thousand in a checking account and one hundred thousand in short-term bonds that could convert to cash quickly. In our conversation with Mr. Schwab, we told him about our new companies being formed. He asked who was handling these. He praised Mr. Burke and thought the Grimes were the best accountants in the area. He also wanted to know who was handling our business insurance.

I've got to give it to Dad. He is cool under fire.

He asked, "We have been looking around. Do you recommend anyone?"

"I am biased, but I think the State Granger Agency is the best. You should know it is my brother who runs it."

"We will check them out," Dad replied.

We walked across the street to the State Granger office. You have to love small towns. John Schwab welcomed us with open arms. His eyes got as big as the moon when we told of our needs.

"You both need a Business Owner's Policy; it will cover business interruption, general liability, crime, vehicle, and property. If you have employees, will you be providing health care? What about individual life policies on yourselves?"

What I thought would be a fifteen-minute stop turned into two hours. I hated this use of my time while on hiatus, but I shudder to think of what could happen if these issues weren't covered. Both my dad and I felt we had dodged a big bullet today.

My Uncle Gene, who runs a dry cleaner, might have told us about these issues. No one else in the family had ever owned a business, at least any who were in contact. It gave me a little insight into how doctors' children became doctors so often, or racecar drivers' kids ended up doing the same. You were born into it, not genetically but by heritage.

It was almost four o'clock, but we had one more stop. I thought we would have been to the Ford dealer by nine this morning. It didn't matter what time we showed up. They were ready to sell a car. It was easy. We walked in. I pointed at the red T-Bird convertible on the showroom floor and said, "This one."

They wanted me to test drive it and show me all the features. Since it was identical to my California car, I ended up showing the salesman how to raise and lower the roof. There was one surprise: the engine was a 352ci. I don't know where I got it wrong. I thought it was a 356ci. I'm glad I got that important point straight. I would've had to turn in my teenage motorhead card.

They wanted to wheel and deal. I told them I would pay exactly what I had paid for the identical car in California. This nonplused the salesman and his manager when they found out I owned a car in California. The manager groaned a little but went with it. They promised the car would be prepped and ready for delivery by six o'clock, right after dinner.

We went home, had dinner, and returned by six o'clock. Wonder of wonders, the car was ready. Dad had written the check, and they had walked it over to the bank, which had it cleared already. You have to love small towns.

I followed Dad home in my new car. It was weird. The car was identical to the one I had in California. The only difference I could tell was this one still had the new-car smell.

Denny, Eddie, and even Mum and Mary were at the door when I arrived at the house. They immediately had to have a ride. I took Mum and Mary first, next Denny and Eddie. We could have all squeezed in if Mary sat on Mum's lap, but we didn't want to do that.

Of course, we had the top down, windows up, and heater on full blast. Mum and Mary were happy with a short ride around the block. Denny and Eddie had to go downtown and out through the pizza drive-through to show off. It was cold enough that no one was out.

I looked forward to attending high school tomorrow morning to check that my California records had arrived. I could go to the office at any time of the day. I decided to go when everyone was arriving. I would like to see my old friends. It's not like I wanted to show off my car or anything. Well, maybe just a little.

I started a book, but I couldn't finish it. Malachi Constant was about as stupid as a rock. Rumfoord's being in a chrono-synclastic infundibulum was interesting, but as a character, he was hopeless. I suppose the author was trying to make a point. By the time I gave up, I was ready to give him the point of my sword.

Chapter 9

Tuesday, I was up at seven-thirty local time. It felt like four-thirty to me. After my morning exercises and run, I took a shower and dressed in what I thought of as my California uniform, slacks, loafers, golf shirt, and sports coat. The shirt was yellow as it showed off my tan. Oh, vanity is thy name.

At breakfast, Eddie and Mary ignored my dress. You could see Denny eyeing me for fashion ideas. Mum thought I looked nice.

Dad was the only honest one there, "Hey, showboat, looking good."

I had to grin at that. He had nailed it.

"Hey, Dad, did you ever call that William Rowland?"

"I did," he replied.

"What was it all about?"

"That note has existed in one form or another for eighty years. The family split around 1900, and they lost track of many members. The only thing they had going was a deed that all the family's senior members had a copy of. The deed had been hidden behind Pio Pico's grave for a while, so they left the box with the note in it. They figured that they could reestablish contact as various family members found it. I called and have been invited to join the La Puente Valley Historical Society, which is undertaking the restoration of both houses. Most members are related to one of the two families, so it is a way to bring them together."

"Are you joining?"

"I think so. Bill Rowland is sending me the application. When you get beyond my brothers, I don't have many relatives. It would be nice to meet someone with common roots."

"I guess so."

"By the way, Rick, don't let your head swell too much when you go to school."

"What do you mean?"

"Your success is far beyond what most kids will ever have. Don't think that makes you better than them."

"I know I'm not better than them, Dad."

"Just don't get caught up in the moment and damage your friendships."

As I drove to school listening to "Venus" by Frankie Avalon on the radio, I thought about what Dad had said. I pulled over and raised the T-Bird's roof. Dad was right; it would be easy to put down my friends. I didn't need the ragtop down for them to know it was a convertible. That would be rubbing it in their faces. The car would speak for itself.

I had planned to be reserved when I entered the building, waiting to see how I was received. I would now be open and greet my friends like people I hadn't seen for a while. I wouldn't be silly about it. I would just act like I had gone on a little vacation and nothing had changed.

That lasted until I was in the parking lot. Kids were eyeing my car as I pulled in. When I got out, anyone who claimed to know me, which was most of the school, came over to check it out. The guys were checking the T-Bird. The girls split between me and the car.

It was so obvious it was almost funny. I answered the guy's questions about the car. "Yes, it's a 352 cubic inch engine. It can go over a hundred, but I haven't tried it yet."

Boy, was I glad the salesman had straightened me out on the engine displacement.

"Hey, Rick," Tom Humphreys started, "you act like you know all about the car, but the sticker is still on the rear window."

I didn't think when I replied, "It is identical to the one I drive in California."

That threw the proverbial cat among the pigeons.

"That's another thing; you aren't old enough for a driver's license."

I had realized the error in letting out that I owned two T-Birds, but as my mother said, "In for a penny, in for a pound."

"The studio helped me with a hardship driver's license. It is good everywhere."

"Some guys have all the luck," said Humphreys, but it was without any heat in it, just a comment.

"On this, I did. They must have figured it was cheaper than providing me with a car and driver. There isn't much in the way of bus, taxi, or train service out there. If you don't have wheels, you have a problem."

As I was saying this, I was moving towards the school's side entrance. Most of the kids were heading that way, so we made a crowd as we went in. I noticed that many of the freshmen in the crowd had growth spurts. The guys were taller and gangly-looking. The girls were filling out.

"Are you returning to class?" someone asked.

"No, they gave us a week off, and I wanted to see my family."

"Are you going to class here this week?" Another person in the group asked.

"I took the California examinations to complete the ninth grade. I'm here to check that the school has my current records."

"So, you are now a tenth grader?"

"I will be when I start classes again."

For some reason, this didn't lead to any more questions. I think everyone knew how I had been doing in school before I left, so they weren't surprised.

The homeroom bell rang to start the school day, so the crowd scattered. I went to the office to check up on my records. I had been told they had been mailed, but confirming their arrival seemed like a good idea. Besides, this was my excuse to be here.

Mr. Gordon, the school principal, was standing at the front counter when I entered the office. He immediately escorted me to his office in a friendly manner. He had all sorts of questions about my educational experience.

I related how it had all been handled, even going into the test proctoring and the attitude. He wasn't surprised to hear it.

"People in situations like yours can feel entitled to a free pass on life. I'm glad to see that isn't your case, Rick."

"I've done extremely well, but there has been a lot of hard work behind it. I know I've been lucky, but at the same time, I was ready to seize the opportunities."

"Rick, would you mind sharing that message with the whole school?"

"No, but how would I do that?"

"I will call a school assembly for the next period. I'm sure there will be many questions about your adventures out in California. I know this will be the topic of discussion all day, and we won't get much teaching done. Add that to the fact that it's March, and everyone is getting tired of school, and that includes the entire staff. A break won't hurt us."

Chapter 10

That is how I found myself center stage in the auditorium. Mr. Gordon introduced me. We agreed on a simple opening statement. I would make a few remarks, most notably being prepared to seize opportunities. I also added that I wasn't super intelligent or anything. I just read the chapter before going to class. That was a trick I learned at Berkeley during my summer vacation.

That vacation was well-known to the student body. It was the stuff of legends. Before I went into any of that on stage, I started with a joke, as speakers were taught to do.

I opened with, "I remember my last trip to center stage. Mr. Hurley, Mr. Gordon, and Mr. Watkins were waiting for me."

This gave me a laugh, as I expected. That was another legend. I also acknowledged the Toms who had been involved. I didn't want to hog the glory, or whatever gets the most massive detention ever given in Bellefontaine school history was considered.

From there, it was open Q&A. As to be expected, most were about Hollywood life and making a movie. I told them the good and the bad, the long hours, getting thrown into a horse trough repeatedly. There were high expectations, and you never wanted John Wayne to chew you out.

There were questions about Paul Grant and how we got along. That was easy. We didn't. He went his way, and I went mine. I only knew him from the set and how he worked harder to get out of his contract than to make a movie. I had no idea about any events off the set. Of course, I said nothing about my beating.

Someone asked about my schooling in California. As they had heard, I finished ninth grade in six weeks, and how come they couldn't? I referred back to seizing the opportunity by being prepared. They could finish school quickly if they studied ahead and had an individual private tutor. In other words, luck and hard work played a big part in it. I wasn't anyone special.

Another person said, "I heard you are rich. Are you?"

"I don't know about rich, but my family is comfortable. For those who don't know, my dad has been able to take advantage of the housing market. He now owns over fifty rental properties in five different cities. Oh, and they pay you well for making a movie."

I think I dodged that bullet. I wasn't ready to go public on the adjustable shower head, designer fixtures, or the hairdryer, much less the money involved.

I was asked if I had a girlfriend. I told them I was partway there as I had a particularly good friend in Nina Monroe. We weren't going steady. I segued from that to the dinner party at her dad's house. I met George Burns, Gracie Allen, and Milton Berle there. One dope wanted to know if Uncle Miltie wore a dress to dinner.

"No!"

The questions went on for the full forty-five-minute assembly. I was surprised when the audience applauded at the end. Miss Bales and Mr. Hurley sought me out as everyone was leaving.

Miss Bales said, "Rick, thank you for that hairdryer. I've never seen anything like it, and why did you send me one? I know nobody but Myron and I received these gifts."

"They are my invention. They will be on sale nationwide within six months. I gave you and Mr. Hurley these gifts as a thank you for the effort and help you gave me in getting to where I am today."

"It seems to be my only help is detention and demanding hard work in class."

"That is exactly what I needed."

"Even the detention?"

"I'm finding that I'm in a dangerous place in life. You helped me keep grounded. Otherwise, I might have become another Paul Grant."

"You are very wise, Rick," responded Miss Bales.

"Not really," I shrugged. "You guys, among others, kept me grounded long enough to figure things out. Even this morning, Dad had to bring me back down to earth. The higher I go, the worse it is going to get. I just hope I don't forget the lessons I've learned."

I then ruined my suddenly somber adult image by asking, "Have you seen my new car?"

"No, we have classes to teach, maybe later."

"Okay. It would be neat to put the top down, blast the radio, and cruise downtown with the two strictest teachers in school."

They both laughed at that. Mr. Hurley said, "I think not. I have an image to protect. It took me ten years to build it, and you want to ruin it in one afternoon."

That's when I realized that these two people weren't only human. They were good people.

I was getting ready to walk out the door when I realized that I hadn't checked to see if my school records had been updated. It turned out they had. Mr. Gordon thanked me for the Q&A session.

He smirked, "It's a shame you'll have to do it all over again.

"What do you mean?"

"George Weaver heard about it. He wants to interview you and some of the other students to see how they received it."

You have to love a small town.

"If I'm going to escape George, I had better run now.'

"Good luck with that. I've never been able to avoid him."

I couldn't either. He was sitting at our kitchen table when I got home. Rather than fight it, I went with the flow. First, I told him how the day had started when I arrived at the school parking lot and how it proceeded from there. I gave him as many of the questions that I had answered as I could. He opened his notebook and told me some things I had forgotten.

I was impressed. I had been on stage an hour ago, and he knew a lot about it. More in some cases than I did.

After reflection, I told him, "Mr. Gordon burned up the phone line getting to you."

"Why do you think it was him?"

"It has happened so fast it had to be someone from the school. He is the only one with a private office and phone, *quod erat demonstrandum*."

"Whatever that means," Mr. Weaver replied.

I ignored that as I figured he was ignoring my statement. It didn't matter.

Mr. Weaver, "I would be interested in how the kids took my presentation. I didn't want to come off as egotistical."

"Rick, from what little I've heard, it is just the opposite. They like you and are glad to see you succeed. It shows them that they can succeed if they apply themselves. That is why I received the phone call. A certain person wants that message out into the community."

"I'll be glad to help."

It took another hour to bring all the information out and what I was trying to say. The whole time, Mum sat there and took it in.

After Mr. Weaver left, she told me she was proud of how I handled myself today.

"Sudden fame can do things to people, most of it bad. You've done well."

I drove down to Don's after school was out and caught up with the Terrible Toms, as they were now called in school. Tom Pew wasn't there, but Wilson and Morton were. Tom Wilson told me that he had straightened up and was having more fun than he did as the class clown.

They both wanted to know the inside scoop on the hot actresses in Hollywood. I crossed my fingers and told them I didn't know any. They would die if they knew I would have dinner with Anna

Romanov tomorrow night. My parents would be there, but so what? It was with Anna Romanov!

The guys would overreact. I had spoken to Miss Romanov often enough now that I was comfortable around her. Still, having her name and number in my little black book was a big deal, not that I would share it.

I did tell them I had introduced Paul Anka and Annette to each other at a party. They both agreed I was stupid. I didn't disagree.

At home later, we played Monopoly as a family. It was nice. Denny drove us all out of business. Mary didn't even get upset.

She said, "He's been hanging around our real-estate-wheeling-and-dealing father for too long."

I guess you had to be there to appreciate the line.

Later in the evening, I started a new thriller. It had a guy awarded the Medal of Honor for saving troops, but they were brainwashed to believe that. He was an assassin for the communists. A queen of diamonds playing card triggered him to receive his instruction. Marco, the hero, figured it out and triggered him with orders to kill his handlers. It was a pretty grim novel.

It was weird because I had read *I, Claudius* not that long ago, and parts of the novel read exactly like that.

Chapter 11

Wednesday had a leisurely start. That meant I had nothing to do until the limo arrived after I started the day. Denny and Eddie were in school, but Mary was home, so we had a tea party. We both were very British in our accents. She was even more of a natural at it than I was. The funny part is that Mum could seldom tell when we did it. It sounded normal to her.

I packed my suitcase for the trip. This was a business trip, so I planned on wearing a suit for all events. I did take the time to try on my Civil War and Scout uniforms to see if they would still fit. The Civil War ones did, but I needed new BSA ones. Mum said she would order them, but I would have to pay a tailor to sew on all the patches.

Dad joined us at lunch. Shortly after that, Mrs. Hernandez came over for Mary. Our limo showed up at the same time. It was being driven by my old friend John Sullivan. It was a stretched-out Cadillac but different from the last time I was in one of theirs.

As John held the door for Mum, I raised an eyebrow at the car. With a wry grin, he nodded and said, "We've won and lost two of them in the last three months. I don't think they use chips anymore." That was worth a chuckle. That had to be one big table!

The arrangement was for John to drive us to Detroit and have a room in the same hotel so that he would be available for the whole trip. He asked what the itinerary would be after we got there. Dad told him that Miss Romanov and two others would be joining us for dinner this evening.

John just said, "Okay."

It was obvious that he had no idea what Dad was talking about. The trip that followed was one of the most interesting I had ever been on, not for the scenery but for what my parents told me.

Mum started it with, "Rick. We decided to wait until you and your siblings were older before we told you this. Now we have decided to tell each of you as you become old enough to understand."

"I had an interesting war, interesting with panzer divisions overrunning the Low Countries and doing an end-run around the Maginot line. I was trapped in France. I was there for the holidays visiting a friend's family. This was in May 1940.

"My friend's father had a short-wave radio which he could use to transmit, which was not so ordinary. At first, the Germans weren't organized, so he could speak to friends in England before we were surrounded. The English managed to smuggle a codebook to him. This was part of the beginning of the French resistance.

"You have to remember that an army is made up of many young men who are away from home and looking for company. My friend Collette and I would attend the German Army gatherings. They would take over a bar and turn it into their nightclub.

"I must say they never mistreated us. They were like young men from everywhere. Collette and I were very chatty. We learned all about them, where they were from, what units they were with, how many of them, where they were going, and whatever else we could pick up. Collette's dad would send this information to England. We were now part of the Stationer Network Division, F for France.

"One of the messages informed me that I was now a member of the Special Operations Executive with the rank of corporal. I would be getting paid, which was nice, but since I was in France, I wouldn't be able to collect it until I got back to England.

"It didn't take long before we saw some opportunities to hinder the Jerry's. We found that we could derail freight trains moving war supplies. After two derailments, they had troops on every train. This was considered a plus as it kept their soldiers from other duties.

"One night by prearrangement, a British bomber dropped our supplies. There were weapons and their munitions, plus a high explosive called Baratol. We didn't know how to use it, so they included a manual. It is a wonder Collette and I didn't blow ourselves up.

"This lasted for almost a year. Things were getting nastier all the time. The Germans would take reprisals against the French for the damage we did. We would set ambushes for the Germans and kill as many as we could. For me, it ended in June 1941. I was wounded in a night raid. I will never wear a two-piece swimming suit.

"They managed to evacuate me to England, where it took me six months to heal. In the meantime, while in the field, I was promoted to sergeant. During my healing time, I was an advisor to the SOE on special operations. Very few of us were in the field. I'm afraid that to the chair-bound warriors, as we called them, I was considered to be extremely uncivilized.

"That reminds me, Pearl Witherington was sent to replace me. We met after the war. She always blamed me for her not getting her parachutist wings. You are required to make five jumps to qualify. She had done three practice jumps when she had to jump into France to replace me. Since she only had four jumps total when the war was over, she was denied her wings.

"To add insult to injury, they denied her the Military Cross because women weren't eligible. She was put in for a Knighthood in the OBE civil division. She turned it down because what they had done wasn't civil at all. After the war, she was awarded the MBE in the military division, so she ended up with a slightly lower award."

Anyway, Mum went on to explain that she was moved to the Secret Intelligence Service, which later became MI6, to a special group trained to be bodyguards for high-level people. She was commissioned as a captain in the Women's Auxiliary Air Force or WAAF. This enabled her to move freely through militarized England without having to show her SIS identification.

Her first assignment was at Bletchley Park to be an escort for the young genius types who worked there when they wanted to go for a night on the town. Her job was to get them out and back without the projects being compromised. They ended up babysitting a bunch of drunks.

"This changed after three months and before I killed anyone," she explained. "I was certainly ready. After a bunch of Germans, what would a drunken grabby Brit or two mean?

"There was a need to escort a member of the royal family as she performed her war duties as an ambulance driver. That is how I met Princess Elizabeth. I was to be her bodyguard of last resort. She was surrounded by most of the army in London, but it was my job to keep her alive, no matter the cost.

"We became good friends. Besides being with her on duty, we ran around together off duty. She loved to go into small pubs where she wasn't known and join in the sing-a-longs with common, normal people. She was a real goer in those days, and I had to chase many a young man away. If they had only known, actually if her dad, King George the VI, had known, they probably would have ended up in the Tower.

"Anyway, a dreadful night came when German spies caught up with us. It was a well-laid trap with inside information. Our ambulance was having what we thought was a wounded man from the blitz loaded into the back when they came at us from the side.

"Fortunately, it was from my side of the car on the left, and I was standing with the door half-closed in front of me. They could not see that I had my Lanchester SMG by my side as I always did.

"When there were unknown men with guns charging at the princess, I wasn't required to give any warnings. I took the three from the side down with a controlled burst. I quickly looked at the back. The two stretcher-bearers were trying to bring weapons to bear but had been delayed by having to set the stretcher down. Again, I didn't ask questions. I just took those two out.

"The man on the stretcher managed to raise his handgun and fired a shot at me, but he had a poor angle and missed. He received the last of the clip in the face."

"I quickly replaced the empty clip in the magazine and checked on Elizabeth.

She was calmly standing there and said, "If you are done here, we had better move on. We'll be late for tea.""

"For that act, I was created Viscountess Jackson. It is a life title; it cannot be inherited and was accompanied by no land or other income, so it doesn't mean much. Since we came to America penniless, I chose not to use it. It is also the reason I've never become a naturalized citizen. I would have to surrender the title, and I just can't do that.

"An interesting side note; with your dual citizenship, you have the courtesy title of The Honorable Richard Jackson. You have that your entire life. It is on your British passport."

"I have a British passport?"

"We keep it in the safety deposit box at the bank, but yes, you do. You were issued one in 1947 when we came over, and it was renewed in 1957. You may remember we had you down to Hadley's studio for a picture. Since you are a minor, it doesn't require your signature. You've never seen it. I'll get it out for you when we get home.

"There is something you must remember. You must never use your British passport at a United States customs point. If you do, you legally surrender your United States citizenship at that moment. You've sworn to a United States official that you are a British citizen, not a U.S. one."

"What about using my U.S. passport at a British point of entry?"

"No problems, the laws are different. Since you weren't born on U.S. soil, you have to declare yourself a U.S. citizen through your father. Being born on English soil makes you a British citizen by birthright, and that cannot change. Your United Kingdom citizenship extends to your children and grandchildren."

"Wow, this is a lot to think about."

"Do you see why we waited until you were older before we told you?"

"Yeah, I get that. I do have a question now that you've got money. What are you going to do?"

"What do you mean?"

"Well, you told me that you didn't use the title because you couldn't live up to the perceived lifestyle. Now you can."

"Richard, now you've given me something to think of."

In stories that have servants, the family forgets that they are present and say things in front of them that they don't want to get out. I had always thought that a weak plot device.

I was so wrong. From the car's front seat came, "Lady Jackson, it mayn't be my place to say, but you should be proud of what you did during the war and the title you earned."

"Oh, John, we forgot you were there. Please don't tell anyone."

"I won't, but it is a good story."

"Peg, in your training, what was taught about keeping secrets?" Dad asked.

"You're right. It is too late now. John, please refer to me as Lady Margaret if you must use my title, and it is no longer a secret."

"Yes, My Lady. I've always wanted to say that."

"Why is it Lady Margaret and not Lady Jackson?" I asked.

"The title is mine, not your dad's. As an American, he cannot hold a title, and in England, the husband of a titled woman holds no title."

"Not even the honorable?"

"Not even."

"Dad, I think you can call me by my title from this day forward."

"In a pig's eye, I will."

"It was worth a try." That would be my first and last joke, bad or otherwise, about a title for some time to come until I saw how things worked out.

"Mum, if you are going to start using your title, may I inform my contacts?"

"Do you mean your friends in the press?"

"Yes, by feeding them tidbits, they've been teaching me how to express things to the rest of the media."

"I wondered about that. You presented yourself very well in interviews recently."

"They've taught me to have a plan in mind for formal interviews and even a prepared statement for ambushes. They call it having 'talking points'. No matter the question, I may turn it into my talking point. If they return with the same question I don't want to answer, I just go back to my talking point. That way, I've some control of the message that gets out.

"I owe that mostly to my friends at the *LA Examiner* and the scandal sheet. The others will take any information I give them, but they are into crime stories, not Hollywood happenings. They use the information I may give them to trade with other reporters for information they want. It's like money in the bank for me, at least I hope so. I do realize they'd turn on me in a heartbeat if it got them a story."

Dad spoke up, "Mr. Sullivan, I trust you will keep some of this quiet. You may freely use the story of Lady Margaret's title, but please keep confidential the rest of this conversation."

"I will not repeat anything, Mr. Jackson. Hearing this is interesting, but sometimes you are better off not knowing, so you won't be tempted. I should have used this feature of the car earlier."

At that, he hit a button, and a window came up between the front and back compartments of the car.

"Damn," my dad said softly. "I should have realized that."

"Too late now, Jack. We'll live with what comes out. It's not too bad. My war story is really old news. The title will be a nine-day sensation in Bellefontaine. If nothing else comes out, the only thing that could harm is publicizing Rick's contacts in the media, and the worst that it would do is shut them down or, more likely, get him more. The downside is his acting peers would be wary of talking to him."

I will say one thing, all this information made the trip go fast!

Chapter 12

We arrived at the hotel around four o'clock, so we had plenty of time to get ready for our six-thirty meeting. There was a message at the front desk for me to call Miss Davis. This was the name in which Miss Romanov had her room reserved. It was the only reason the lobby wasn't jammed with reporters and fans.

I called her and asked if we could meet in the lobby before dinner. We later found a quiet corner, and I found out that she had concerns about dinner and the tour tomorrow. She had never been to a factory and wanted to know how to behave. I assured her that dinner would be an informal gathering of nice people.

I did share with her the history of Detroit Faucet and how I had become involved with them. She seemed impressed that I had invented an adjustable shower faucet and later a hairdryer. I had read up on the early history of DF and how it had descended to Mark and his sister. Mum had written to Mark and found out about the awards Sally Enright had won.

This all went towards making Ms. Romanov less nervous. I could hardly believe that I was comforting a person who was considered the epitome of aplomb. This went to show how great an actress she is.

She did tell me she had her pictures ready to go.

"What do you mean your pictures are ready to go?"

"My most recent publicity still, that I have personally autographed, with a space to insert people's names."

"That's a good idea. I probably should have some."

"Your studio liaison hasn't set you up with some?"

"No, this is the first I knew of them."

"You better take care of that when you get home."

I did more than that. I made a panic call to Mark Downing and asked if he could arrange a photographer for tomorrow. I was lucky the plant purchasing agent was an amateur photographer who did work on the side and was supposedly rather good.

He did weddings for employees without complaints. I asked him to arrange for him to be available tomorrow for the tour. Mark thought that was an excellent idea.

We didn't talk long as he had to make the call and come to the hotel to meet us before dinner.

We all met in the lobby at the appointed time and left for the Caucus Club at 150 W. Congress (on the first floor of the Penobscot Building). Mark directed John Sullivan to the restaurant. I couldn't find it again if I had to.

The food was wonderful. The company was great. Listening to Anna, it was hard to believe she was the nervous person of several hours ago. She used the information I had given her to present herself as a knowledgeable and interested person. It didn't come across as fake. Her knowledge may be recent, but her interest was real.

Sally Enright was what I would call a normal person. She was a well-dressed twenty-something and presented herself well. She wore a modest engagement ring which became the center of discussion among the ladies. This broke the ice for all of us.

Miss Romanov explained that she intended to come up with her line of houseware products and sell them in all major retail outlets. Her financial advisors told her that two events were about to change the American retail landscape: credit and television.

Last year, a bank had sent out sixty thousand unsolicited cards in California. These were called credit cards. Merchants would accept these instead of cash. Before this, it was cash or check only. The credit would be obtained from a bank or loan company. Some of the larger stores would have revolving accounts available at their location.

Now that credit was available, the American public could release the enormous pent-up demand for consumer goods that had built up during the Depression, World War II, and the Korean Conflict. The people were tired of self-denial. As to what people would buy, television advertising would tell them what they should buy.

It appeared to her that the DF project was the perfect time and place for her to get involved. This information left me thinking about how lucky I was. I needed to obtain some education in this because luck can change.

The meal took three hours. The restaurant had excellent service, and the food was wonderful. They let us eat in peace and didn't try to turn the table. This was a class act. The check and the tip reflected all of this.

Before the meal ended, the ladies took the conversation in a different direction.

Sally Enright started it by asking, "Miss Romanov, what sort of advertising campaign are you planning to use to start your business?"

"I plan to start with the TV special about Ricky since DF will get its initial exposure there, but as to a theme, I don't have one yet."

From there, the ladies talked of possible ads that could be run, everything from a Busby Berkeley extravaganza to the hunky guy without a shirt. They took turns describing the guy. When it was Mum's turn, I wanted to die of embarrassment. Mums aren't supposed to think like that!

Miss Romanov turned serious. "The famous endorsement would always work. I could get some other actress or notorious woman, even a noblewoman, to be my first customer."

I had to open my mouth, "What about using Lady Margaret Viscountess Jackson?"

Dad laughed. Mum shuddered.

"Rick, when I said I would start using the title. I didn't mean today!"

Of course, the whole story had to come out. That is the real reason the dinner took so long. When it got to Pearl Witherington, Miss Romanov burst into that throaty laughter she was noted for.

"You're the one! Pearl has moaned about you getting wounded for years. She didn't get her parachutist wings because of you."

This led us to adjourn back to the hotel to its restaurant, where with coffee and tea in hand, they now played do you know and were you there when. Mum and Miss Romanov were close to the same age. Dad, Mark, Sally, and I sat and listened.

In England, they would say, "I could dine out on the stories for years."

Miss Romanov at one point said, "Pearl told me that you were the deadliest person she had ever met. That you killed the enemy as fast as possible and with no remorse."

"Stuff and nonsense, I killed the Germans by the hundreds. Pearl organized hundreds of men to kill the Germans by the thousands."

"Her point was that you did it yourself."

"That may be true, but she still was the more effective warrior."

I made eye contact with Dad, but he just brushed it off. None of this was news to him. Mark and Sally had eyes as wide as teacup saucers.

"As far as remorse, it was war. There is no remorse in war, revulsion at what has to be done and the outcome, but no remorse. War is war. Destruction of the enemy's will to fight is the goal. Not their ability to fight. As long as they have rocks and are alive, they can fight.

"I don't understand the Americans and Korea. They've left an enemy at their back. If this becomes a national habit, there will come a day when they direly regret it."

That little tirade by Mum was a conversation killer. Shortly after that, we ended the evening. We agreed to meet in the lobby at 7:30

a.m.; that was the time John Sullivan had been told. Sally and Mark made their goodbyes and left for their respective homes.

I didn't read but didn't fall asleep quickly. I learned many things today about my mum. It was a shock to find she had the title of nobility. To find out she could be a bloodthirsty killer was beyond shock. Various thoughts, like her recent trip to England, kept trying to coalesce, but I suppressed them.

My sleep was restless.

A good run and a long shower in the morning helped a lot. About a gallon of coffee later, I was ready to face the day. Everyone else looked well-rested. Mr. Sullivan drove us over to the Detroit Faucet Corporation.

The building itself was an enormous pile of brick typical of that built in the late nineteenth century. Mark had outdone himself. There were welcome banners up in the lobby for Miss Romanov and Viscountess Jackson. That was quick work.

He had his photographer there who followed us the whole day. Before the day was done, every employee in the plant had posed with Mum and Miss Romanov. Dad and I were bystanders to this show.

The plant was cleaned. I had never been to a facility that did forging before but knew that this cleanup had been recent. Again, Mark showed his business acumen by having Sally reveal the first designs for the DF and Romanov collections to us. Miss Romanov told us she couldn't wait to see them.

"Then come this way," said a proud Mark.

He took us to the forging area. There, a workman showed us how hand-carved wooden models of the faucet and knob were packed in a frame filled with sand to produce a reverse casting. The sand was "fixed" with some chemical, and then molten metal was poured into the mold.

From there, the new casting was put in a tumbler with fine gravel to remove the dross. Next was a trip to the machine shop, where the holes were bored and threaded where needed. Lastly, we went to the electro-plating shop where the new faucet was nickel-plated.

It took the better part of two hours, but in the end, Miss Romanov was presented with the first faucet for her new collection.

Upon receiving the faucet, she remarked, "I have a lighted shelf at home with two Oscars. This will be placed in between them."

To say the day went well was putting it mildly. There was a catered lunch for the whole plant. As I suspected, not much work was getting done. I had a few minutes to talk to Mark Downing. We had just met but were getting along well. He was in his early thirties.

He told me, "I can't wait for the next family dinner. My sister thinks she is better than the rest of the family and that she is too good to be in such a mundane business as faucets. I will have the photo album from today with me."

Later in the afternoon, we dropped Miss Romanov off at the airport for her flight home. We were quiet on the drive back to Bellefontaine. We were all lost in our thoughts.

I had a question for Mum but decided I would never ask it.

Friday and Saturday at home were nice. I spent time with my brothers and sister. Friday night, I went to the youth center and was with my friends, but we didn't have much to talk about anymore. My life wasn't better than theirs. It was different.

Tracy, Tom's old girlfriend, told us how her mother had been on a TV game show in Dayton, won a new sofa, and spent time with the host, a local celebrity in Dayton.

It wouldn't be cool to follow that with, "Oh. I spent the last two days with Anna Romanov."

So, I didn't talk much.

Chapter 13

Sunday, I flew to Denver to be in position for Monday's filming. The studio had a bus arranged since many of us came in at the same time.

Monday, I woke up a little disoriented. It didn't take long to figure out where I was. I had been here before. It still was a little strange waking up in the guest room at the Easterly ranch. Last evening, when I arrived, the studio had an Airstream travel trailer waiting for me since I was one of the stars. The Easterlies would hear none of that. I was their friend and would stay in the guest room.

The Airstream was good, but a real bed was better. Especially when all the beds in the house were longer than normal because of Mr. Easterly's height. At six feet five inches, he was taller than me. These beds beat Airstream by a wide margin.

It was still way early, so I quietly put on my running gear and did my morning workout outside. When I got back from my run, I saw a light in the barn, so I knew Mr. Easterly was doing the morning chores. I went over and pitched in. No pun intended, but I was using a pitchfork to pick up the straw and manure.

We had been at it for about ten minutes, silently working away, when Mr. Wayne entered the door. He found another pitchfork and helped. Okay, I will quit pitching the bad jokes. Anyway, he helped with no fuss at all.

We were almost finished when Dusty Rhodes, one of the writers, stuck his head in the door to see what was going on. He took one look and took off like a scalded cat. I don't think he wanted to get involved in cleaning out the last of the horse stalls.

I was wrong because he soon returned with Mr. Dodge.

Ron got all excited. "You're right," he told the writer, "This is what we need."

He then explained to us that they were short some material on Sir Nicklaus doing menial chores below him. At the same time, John Wayne would be doing the work as part of his daily routine.

Mr. Dodge looked around and saw that we were almost done.

"Round up the crew, and we'll have them spread this stuff to get some shots this morning."

"Hold on a minute," said Mr. Easterly. "That just isn't common sense. Wait until tomorrow morning. The horses will spread the 'stuff,' as you call it. They don't need our help."

Even Mr. Dodge had the grace to laugh. "Yeah, that works. It will give the lighting and camera crews time to set up."

After makeup, we all got in the saddle; today, it was pictures of us riding. Riding alone, riding in a group, chasing and being chased. My girlfriend and I rode to a picnic, chased by outlaws, riding for help, riding to help, you name it, and we were riding somewhere for something.

I had been riding regularly since the beginning of filming, but nothing like this. I would get through the day, but I knew that I would pay when I got off the horse this evening. During the day, I was rotated through four horses that had the same coloring. You don't want to wear the animals out, you know. There were people on-site to protect the animals today. I wish we poor actors had the same protections.

Lunch was a box lunch. The food was good, and the conversation was better. We had been on hiatus for a week. You would've thought it was back to school after three months off. People were moving from table to table, asking each other what they had done. I only told people that I spent time with my family. It would've been too difficult and premature to talk about my trip to Detroit.

I did let them know I had made a trip to my high school. The guys got the biggest kick out of this.

"I bet you were the big man on campus" was the common comment.

When I explained how I went to lengths to avoid that, they nodded and made sounds like they thought it was the right thing to do. Somehow, I didn't believe them. After a while, I wondered why I hadn't put on an act.

Well, not really, but I did choose to miss an opportunity. From my viewpoint, it made a lot of sense. To the horny guys on the crew, I missed my chance. Anyway, we all talked and caught up with each other. We were told that we would be having a Western barbeque for dinner.

We ended the riding scenes on schedule, so I thought I had a couple of hours to kill before dinner. Sammy approached me with a long, thin object wrapped in cloth. It was an English longbow. Rod Bell had sent it along. There was also a quiver with twenty-five of the yard-long arrows.

I was to bend and loose the bow one hundred times a day. Sammy borrowed straw bales from Mr. Easterly. It was a strain when I bent the bow the first time.

Sammy laughed. "It is a ninety-pound bow. Rod was certain you could handle it."

I could, but it took a real effort.

I wasn't any better at hitting the target than before. Sammy told me after my first ten thousand shots, I would see an improvement. The next steps after that were at one hundred thousand and again at a million. I knew then I would never be considered a skilled archer.

At the end of the day, it was as I had predicted, or as they say in the Old West, I was just plumb tuckered out. That didn't prevent me from overeating at the barbeque. With the large crew present, it was decided to cook out as much as possible. The caterers had to bring in everything from Denver, which was almost a four-hour drive.

I didn't understand that we were supposed to be in Wyoming with the foothills of the Rocky Mountains in view. I asked and was told they would be added in later. The advantages of this ranch and its facilities, especially for the rodeo scenes on Wednesday and Thursday, far outweighed doing it in Johnson County. They would add in the foothills in postproduction. Since none of the movie scenes took place in the foothills, they didn't have to worry about them.

Clint and Sally Easterly fussed over me like a long-lost son. They wanted to know about all my activities since I had last seen them. It took several hours to relate the events. They were more interested in the business side of things than the movie. They informed me that I had created a small industry in Craig.

The bank moved to another location. The local historical society rented the old bank and charged people to see the reenactment of the bank robbery. According to Mr. Easterly, their interpretation of events was a little loose, but the people were paying to see it. They had a gift shop. You could even get your picture taken with a cardboard cutout of hero Ricky Jackson.

I liked the entrepreneurial spirit. I wasn't certain how sound their business model was. I decided if I got a chance, I would get into Craig and take a look. I don't see how that robbery could be billed as exciting. It was started and finished in seconds.

That night I read one of the paperbacks I bought at the Denver airport. I normally would have never considered it, but the shelves were so thin in the material I took what I could find.

Sylvester, the Duke of Salford, was about as arrogant as a man towards women as possible. At the opening of the story, the duke decided it was time to marry. His mother wouldn't give him any possible names as he held women in very cynical regard. Through his godmother, he meets her granddaughter Phoebe.

As he characterized her, she came across as insipid and talentless. This may be because she knew his reputation and wanted to stay far away. In her "other" life, she is an authoress who has written a satire about English high society. Her main villain is the Duke of Salford! From there, the story goes on with misunderstandings one after the other.

The duke finds out Phoebe wrote the book *The Lost Heir* in which she practically accuses him of murdering his twin brother and kidnapping his nephew. As with all drawing-room comedies, it ended up happily with the duke and Phoebe together after she was kidnapped by Sir Nugent Fotherby and taken to France.

It was a light read, and I finished it that evening. I did idly wonder if my godmother would recommend one of her granddaughters to me. Now that would be something!

Chapter 14

Tuesday morning started like yesterday, except the lighting crew had set up the barn and cameras were in place. Costume had me in an outfit that would've been appropriate for an English countryside outing. It was not what you should wear for shoveling manure! I was a little put out by this scene, to tell the truth.

It had me acting like the privileged kid who was too good to shovel manure. This scene wouldn't have come into being if I hadn't been helping with the real work! Talk about no good deed goes unpunished.

The low point was when I had to smart off to my uncle, Big Jim. He tossed a pitchfork of straw and manure all over me. I don't know what Mr. Easterly feeds his horses, but it is nasty after being processed.

That scene alone took nine retakes. That meant I had to clean up nine times. Twice I required a full shower. Whenever I got hit with a load, I reminded myself what I was making. Note to self—close eyes and mouth when someone is shoveling manure in your direction.

Before I could eat lunch, I had to take a third shower and change clothes. My hairdryer certainly got its workout. They had my hair longer than I usually wore it for the movie. It wasn't the Prince Valiant look, but close. They were saving scenes at the end of the movie where my hair would be cut shorter.

I was done for the day as far as shooting. They wanted me available in the evening for some lighting checks and walkthroughs, but I had four hours free. I looked up Mr. Easterly, which wasn't hard as he had his own director's chair on the set, and asked him if he could run me into town to see the Bank Robbery in Craig as it was billed.

He had nothing going on, and there wasn't any action to watch, so he was glad to run me in. It was only a fifteen-minute drive. The old bank had large signs advertising the Bank Robbery in Craig. See the reenactment and buy your souvenirs, not what you would call subtle.

During the day, they performed the robbery once an hour. We bought a ticket and looked into the old conference room where I had waited for the FBI. This was now the souvenir shop. I couldn't help it. I bought my brothers and sister t-shirts. Of course, they had Bank Robbery in Craig across the front.

You could buy caps and cap pistols, but I couldn't see the connection. They weren't like the weapons used. Mum got a dishtowel with the Bank Robbery in Craig on it. Dad rated a coffee mug. I had my picture taken by the photographer on duty next to the life-size cut-out of Ricky Jackson.

At this point, I realized that I had grown two or three inches since that picture had been taken, so life-size wasn't life-size anymore. That and my haircut were enough that I wasn't recognized. None of those present were around on the day of the robbery.

At the appointed time, with all the spectators in a roped-off area, the show, now designated The Great Bank Robbery in Craig, started. It appeared real as a line of customers accumulated at a bank teller's window. The kid who was playing me looked nothing like me at all. He was dressed in a Western outfit. He was only five-foot-ten at the most and scrawny at that.

I guess that wasn't so bad, but what happened next was so unreal. The two "Johnson" boys burst into the bank, shooting six guns and cap pistols like those in the souvenir shop. They lined everyone up and demanded "your money or your life." I (the re-enactor) jumped the first one and wrestled his gun away from him.

The other turned his gun towards "me", and I shot him, and his gun fell on the floor. It was near the one I wrestled it away from. The one now without a gun went for the gun and aimed it at me. I shot him also. Now, they both took five minutes to make dying speeches about how wrong they were and were sorry for what they had done.

The acting was so terrible it was funny. I looked at Mr. Easterly, and then he looked at me. We didn't giggle. Men don't giggle. It sure sounded like it, though. Then, leave it to a kid about nine or ten. He had a picture of me, a fairly recent one. He was showing it to his mother and pointing at me.

She looked at the picture, then me. She approached me and asked, "Are you Ricky Jackson?"

"Yes, ma'am."

She introduced herself. Holding out the picture and a pen, she asked, "May we have your autograph? Jay is a fan of yours."

"Certainly, Mrs. Leno, I would be glad to sign for Jay."

I wrote on it, "Jay, you will be a star someday," and signed it, "Your future fan Ricky Jackson."

Young Jay asked me, "Is this how it happened?"

By that time, the other ten or so people who had been watching the show had gathered around. There was also a nervous-looking show director. I raised one eyebrow in his direction. He mouthed a silent please towards me.

"Yes, Jay, this is exactly how it happened, give or take a lie or two."

"Neat!"

A look towards the show director got me a mouthed "Thank you."

The photographer approached me and asked if he could get a picture of me with the cast. I couldn't say no at this point, so it became pictures all around. Just when I thought I was away free, the chief of police showed up.

It was the same police chief as when the robbery occurred. We talked for a few minutes. Next thing you know, we were over at the station house with more pictures being taken. At least none of them were mug shots!

When that finished up, I received a surprise request from Mr. Easterly.

"I go to the diner down the street for coffee almost every morning. They are good folks. Can we stop in there?"

"Of course, Mr. Easterly," I replied.

That stop was more than worth it; they had the best coconut cream pie in the world. I had to suffer through two pieces, and the cook insisted on wrapping the rest of the pie to take back to the set. Now my picture will be on the wall with other local celebrities. This was a small enough price to pay for Mr. Easterly's care of me during my visits to this area.

Stuffed to the gills with pie, we headed back to the ranch. There was a set of weights that someone had brought along, so I worked out with those. Then Sammy showed up with the bow. It was a strain, but I managed to shoot all one hundred times today. Yesterday my arms gave out around ninety.

I was shooting into a wall of hay. Yesterday we found out that those arrows would go completely through a bale with a ninety-pound bow. We had to stack them three bales thick as a backstop. Even then, half the length of the arrow was sticking out the back.

Due to my inaccuracy, the wall of hay was not only three deep; it was six bales wide and six bales high for a whole lot of hay. This was at fifty yards. I shuddered to think of the spread I would leave at two or three hundred yards.

By the time I was done with that, someone was beating on the iron triangle that was used to call people to lunch or dinner on the ranch. It had been an hour since pie, so I was hungry again. They were carving up a steamship round of beef and all the fixings tonight. Since I had the pie earlier, I could only make two trips through the serving line.

Tonight, I sat with Ellen Shelly, the female lead, and her mother, Sharon. They were wonderfully comfortable with the ranch life as this is similar to their farm in California. Ellen told me she would go to Craig tomorrow to see the reenactment of the Great Robbery.

I sputtered a bit and told them not to believe everything in the show. It took me a few moments to figure it out. They had heard all about my trip today and were pulling my leg. Even with them being so mean, I offered to share my pie.

By the time they took theirs, I barely got a small piece, and then Mr. Wayne showed up. Oh well, I now knew where it came from. I may have to make a trip to town tomorrow.

After dinner, I took a walk out into a field. It was a clear night, and there were so many stars visible. I wondered if humans would ever get out there. The more I thought of it, I had to find some way to become involved. I was tired after that, so I fell asleep early on a full stomach. That is supposed to make you dream. If so, I don't remember.

Chapter 15

I woke up Wednesday, looking forward to the day. We would be shooting scenes for a rodeo that Sir Nick had entered at his girlfriend's insistence. I wouldn't be doing any of this as the insurance people would have a hissy fit. It would still be fun to watch the professional stunt riders work. I was a gifted amateur; now to see the real men ride.

After my morning workout and run, I stopped in and gave Mr. Easterly a hand with mucking out. We were the only ones there. There isn't much romance in shoveling...stuff.

The breakfast was really good. I had worked up an appetite, so I loaded up with pancakes, bacon, eggs, orange juice, and coffee. Over the second cup of coffee, an assistant director briefed me on my day. It would be shots of me getting on horses and bulls as though I were about to ride them. The actual riding would be by the stunt crew.

My takes were all done by noon. After a light lunch, I returned to the corral where the stuntmen were riding. They completed the roping events. Now, they were getting into what I considered the real thing, riding Brahma Bulls. They had three stunt riders and four bulls, so it shouldn't take long.

First, they got shots of Sir Nick's rodeo competition. It took a lot more takes than I thought it would. They wanted several successful rides and a few failures. They had failures with no problem. It took all three riders using three of the bulls for fifteen rides to get takes of two successful ones.

I was watching this when Mr. Easterly sidled up to me.

"Ricky, I'm going to have to call this off soon. These bulls can only take so much stress."

"It's not good," I agreed.

"I see they are going to try the last fresh bull with the guy dressed like you. Is it Bulldozer?"

"Yeah, they are getting ready, and it is Dozer."

"Why don't we walk over and see how he is setting up."

That would be interesting to see how you settled yourself in and started being told what sort of a ride you would have.

When we got there, I could see that it wouldn't be a good ride. The stuntman was plain tentative. It was as though he was scared of the bull. That's a surefire way to have a bad ride.

It would be a bad ride in the sense of being thrown off and trampled to death.

I said, "Here, back off the bull for a second. I want to check something out."

The stunt man gladly rose from the bull he was about to drop down onto and ride. I took his place. Before anyone realized it was me, I had slammed down onto the bull and gave the signal, and we were off.

It had been a while, but I hadn't lost it. I even managed to wave my hat. After my eight seconds, I slid off and away from the bull while the outriders got him headed back to his pen.

"Once more," shouted the director. "It looked good, but I need another for insurance."

Ouch, bad choice of words for me. He meant insurance, as in losing the film. Insurance, to me, meant the butt-chewing I would probably get.

As Mum would say, "In for a penny, in for a pound."

My second ride was even more spectacular than my first. The bull almost tossed me, and I was in midair, only connected by my hand on the rope. I landed okay and kept my balance for the rest of the eight seconds. Nine and I would have been gone.

Someone must have realized what was going on because I heard a bellow.

"Ricky Jackson, get your butt over here."

Mr. Wayne didn't sound happy. I just thought I had learned some new words when I heard those guys chewed out for not knowing their lines. At least they were only accused of carnal relations with goats.

I heard about the whole zoo. He may have missed aardvarks, but that would have been it. I thought he was throwing his hat on the ground and stomping on it a bit. I took off running when I realized he was winding up for a swing.

Unfortunately, I can run long and far, but I'm not quick. He caught me, and you guessed it, right next to a horse trough. I took another bath, and so did he. I managed to take him with me. That's how that scene got in the movie. They left the zoo and started with him stomping his hat.

It is hard to stay mad when you are soaking wet. It is probably the only reason I'm alive.

As he began to walk away, Mr. Wayne turned to me and said, "Nice riding, Ricky."

The director decided he didn't need any more takes. There was enough footage to work with. The stunt riders searched me out as I was changing into dry clothes.

"That was impressive, Rick. Where did you learn to ride like that?"

"Right here at this ranch. Mr. Easterly taught me the hard way. He got me on a bull to see if I would fall off. I managed to hang on, and the rest is history."

The older stuntman said, "I heard you did some riding, but not that you were any good. I just thought that you had done some small-town rodeo riding."

"I'm still the National Junior Champion."

"Dang that Dick Wyman. He had bets with all of us, that you would outride us. You're a ringer! I didn't think there was any way some young kid could do it better." He continued, "And I learned about what aardvarks could get into."

Trust me. You don't want to know.

Since he and the other guys were laughing, I didn't feel a need to flee the scene. We settled in and traded rodeo stories for a while. It was fun talking to people with the same experiences I had. Few people have lived in the rodeo world, so this was a rare opportunity for me. I was not an expert in it, but I could still understand the stories they were telling.

We all agreed there was no one braver at the rodeo than the clowns. They rushed into harm's way on foot to keep the riders safe. It was dangerous enough to be out there on horseback. To be on the ground was insane.

That made me ask, "Why aren't there any clowns available when you are working?"

"I guess they don't think we are worth it," said the older stuntman with a shrug.

That had me riled up a little, and it was the bad luck of the safety coordinator who also minded insurance matters that he caught up with me. He thought he was going to be able to threaten me with all sorts of dire events for violating safety policy and jeopardizing the insurance coverage.

Man, that was a mistake on his part. I could work off my frustration with Mr. Wayne's chewing out, which I entirely deserved from the safety coordinator.

I told him that I had committed two violations of the policy while he allowed fifteen others to go on. Having no safety people in the form of clowns around to save the riders surely violated our insurance policy.

"As a matter of fact, why don't we go find Producer Saul Goldman right now?"

He lost interest in the whole discussion. He mumbled about having to keep things in order as he walked away. I was pleased with myself. I had turned the subject from me to him and didn't have to bring any mammals into the conversation.

It was getting later in the afternoon, so I headed over to where the archery butts were set up. Sammy was there and had the heavier bow I had used yesterday out and ready for me to string. I managed to do it without tripping over my legs, so I felt like I had accomplished something.

The pull didn't seem any easier, but I was beginning to get the technique. It took a combination of strength and technique. I had the strength but no technique. The practice was helping. Today, I was proud of myself. I hit the wall of hay with every arrow. Notice I said the wall, not the target.

I had one in four in the target and one in the second ring. That shot was where my nose itched, and I thought I had messed up. My arms felt like dishrags at the end of the session.

Sammy asked me after the session how good I wanted to get. "The best as I can, I guess."

"That will take some years. You are good enough now that you can do everything required in the movie. Better than this takes practice, lots of practice. I told you a million arrows. So far, you have shot maybe three hundred."

"I enjoy this. Why don't we keep it up? I would like to be able to hit the target most of the time and also at further distances."

"Accuracy requires the most practice. Distance is more dependent on eyesight. If you can hit it at fifty yards, then three hundred yards is just elevating the bow with the ability to judge the angle. That part is more practice, I guess."

The weights weren't in use so I could do some of my lifts. I ate dinner with Ellen and Sharon. They were peaceful to be around. Ellen told me I was crazy to ride that bull.

"Ellen, I'll share a secret. I learned how to ride bulls on this ranch. I have ridden the Bulldozer as he is known before.

"There is a trick to riding him. If you lower yourself lightly on his back, he feels he has to throw you off immediately. If you slam yourself onto him, he seems to take a few seconds to decide to throw you off. All you have to do is stay on for eight seconds, so a two-second buffer works wonders."

"It still seems dangerous to me," she replied.

"Okay, it was dangerous. Do I get a kiss for my bravery?"

"You know I have a boyfriend; you get a kiss in your dreams or on the set."

"I know, but it was worth a shot."

Her mother Sharon came out with, "Well, dear, if you aren't interested...."

"Mother!" Ellen yelped.

That set us all off laughing. I enjoyed my time with them. It was a little lonely being the youngest on the set.

That night, I read a little in a book on how stocks work. I was interested in the mechanics of an Initial Public Offering (IPO). Not that it would be happening for a long time, but I found it interesting.

Chapter 16

I was up at my usual time on Thursday. Again, after my run and workout, I helped Mr. Easterly with his morning chores. We had a good chuckle about yesterday's bull riding.

As he put it, "Dang fools worry about safety then ask some half-trained guys to try it. Though I guess if they got hurt, it would be less expensive than if you did. That's a sad way to look at life."

"Yes, it is. I hope I never fall into the trap of putting money before people."

"Just keep thinking like that, Rick, and you won't."

I think that was the first time he had ever called me Rick. I noticed people who thought of me as a kid called me Ricky. Those who thought I was a young adult used Rick. My mum and Anna Romanov were the ones who used Richard and Mum only when I was about to catch it.

It's like I had to earn my name. I started to wonder about guys who were called by their childhood nicknames their whole life. There would be Tommy, Tom, and Thomas; Chucky, Charlie, and Charles; there could be Sammy, Sam, and Samuel. I guess most guys had to earn their names.

My stage name is Ricky Jackson. Would it always be that, or would my name grow if I got more serious parts? Hey, I haven't had any coffee yet. I can think odd thoughts.

I had breakfast with the Easterlies in their kitchen. I was invited in, and it was very pleasant. Mr. Easterly and his wife had sheltered me when I needed it, and I would always have a warm place in my heart for them. More practically, I planned to leave my hairdryer with Mrs. Easterly. I had another in California.

I asked how life was treating them. It seemed to be fairly good right now. The ranch was doing fine, and it being used as a location was the whipped cream on top of the sundae as far as they were concerned. I asked them if they planned to sell souvenirs at the bank in town.

"Like what, Ricky?" inquired Mrs. Easterly. She is a motherly type; we grow up slower for them.

"Maybe pictures of the ranch, t-shirts with the movie name. Set up a movie tour in town, like where the crew ate at the dinner. Have a John Wayne pie on the menu? He certainly ate enough apple pie to merit a name on it. Set up a room in the bank to have continuous showings of the movie. Use your imagination."

"Hmm, we will have to give that some thought."

"Rick, are you ready for the cattle drive today?"

"Yes, I'm looking forward to it. The only time I was involved with a lot of cattle was that rustling incident down in Texas."

"Be careful out there. Don't let yourself be caught on foot in the middle of the herd. They weigh so much they could hurt you badly just milling around. If the herd stampedes, which isn't likely, get the heck out of the way. You can't stop them, but they can kill you."

"Do you think there is a possibility?"

"There is always a possibility. Think about it. There are going to be noisy trucks with cameras on them moving around them all day. One crazy cow thinks that it's a monster out to get her, and they all will be running. Taking those cows five miles today and back tomorrow will cause them to lose weight. I'm renting them out for two thousand dollars for the two days and hope to break even."

"You going to be selling movie steaks from those cattle later?" I asked.

"Now, there is an idea. You ought to be in business. I bet you could make your first million by the time you are twenty."

"You think so?" I asked wide-eyed.

"Sure...son of a gun, you've already done it."

"Yes, how did you know?"

"Don't play poker, is all I can tell you."

Keeping with the movie's theme, I moseyed on to make-up. They put some heavy black stuff on my eyebrows and lipstick on me so my face would show up in the harsh sunlight. Costuming had my gear ready. The studio weapons man had my revolver. It hadn't any cartridges in the chamber, but there were blanks in my belt loops.

I asked him why I didn't have dummies in my belt loops.

He winked and said, "Rabid coyotes."

Now that was something to settle my nerves for the day.

I must have looked confused because he added. "Rick, we don't think it is safe to have live weapons around, but at the same time, we feel more comfortable if responsible people are armed. This country can turn dangerous quickly. By the way, those aren't blanks."

"Oh, I won't load them unless it's needed."

"And that, my young friend, is why you have them. The insurance people wouldn't like it, but I have to make the best call on the ground."

Of course, I immediately had the urge to load my gun. I resisted. I didn't resist checking everyone else who carried a gun on the set to see if they had dummies or live ammo. It didn't take long to figure out that Mr. Wayne and I were the only actors carrying real bullets.

Our horses were saddled and waiting for us. That is one nice thing about the movies. They have horse wranglers to do all the work for you. I wondered if I could find a car wrangler to take care of my T-Birds. Now that is a crazy thought. I own two T-Birds. I was more impressed with that than the money.

We finally got the cattle moving. Our four hundred head was more than most movie cattle drives had. It would make for some good scenes. There were six of us driving cattle plus a cook and Lilly, my movie girlfriend, acting as the cook's helper.

It was slow work getting the cattle all moving together in the same direction. We did have to herd them. It wasn't so bad after the herd had sorted out its leaders, and the leaders were moving in the correct direction.

There was no acting here. We were driving cattle. With yips and yells, we kept them moving while at the same time heading off any that tried to go their own way. In the meantime, the cameras mounted on the back of small pickup trucks were buzzing around like flies. They were getting as much footage as they could have of all of us. Of course, they spent more time around Mr. Wayne and me than the others.

This helped kick up more dust. That's when I realized that those bandanas cowboys wore served a purpose. I wasn't allowed to wear one since it would hide my face. It took us all day to drive that herd five miles to a small pond. We set up for the night. I always laughed when I heard the term bedded the cattle down. It brought up pictures of tucking them in bed. It was almost that bad getting them settled down. Some wanted to keep moving.

Once those beasts moved, they didn't stop where you wanted them to. Then some of them would decide they needed to wander over the hill to see if they had greener grass. Finally, they were circled and calmed down for the night.

Almost all the technical crew left for the main ranch in the trucks. One camera truck was left behind for "just in case" camera shots. I was the only cast member remaining behind. I thought it would be cool to have the whole experience. There were four ranch hands, one who acted as the cook, and me.

We had a campfire, and it was really neat being served from the chuck wagon. We had blankets and used our saddles as pillows. It didn't take long to settle down for the evening. I fell asleep early. It turned out to be a good thing.

I woke up when the first raindrops hit my face. Later, I found out it was around two in the morning. The real foreman called loudly for all of us to get up and get dressed. I wondered why he was concerned but didn't question his orders.

The cameraman came over to me. "I'm not sure what's up, but I'm going to start shooting some footage. After the foreman gives his orders, you give the same ones; those will be what is on film, and maybe we will be able to use it."

I quickly passed this idea to the foreman, who nodded in a distracted way.

"What is your concern?"

"Look to the west. We have a big storm coming in. It's the lightning I'm afraid of. We could have a stampede."

At that, he ordered all of us to saddle up. The cameraman and his driver took the hint and got in their truck.

We had about fifteen minutes until we felt the gusts preceding the storm. The rain doused the remains of the fire. The chuckwagon was closed up, and everything was tied down as much as possible. After we were all saddled up, many horses were still on the tie-down line.

After saddling my horse, I took a minute and loaded my revolver. Somehow, I felt I might need it.

One of the hands was stationed there to release all the horses if the cattle did stampede in that direction. As these orders were being given, I mirrored them for the camera. I felt like a fool but understood why I had to do it.

Thunder and lightning were getting closer to us all the time. The cattle were getting restless, and their lowing and mooing sound was almost deafening. Four hundred heads can make a lot of noise.

Then it happened. Lightning struck near enough that I could only count to two before the thunderclap arrived. It was not a clap; it was more like a Civil War cannon going off in your ear. Everything seemed frozen in place for several seconds, and then all hell broke loose. The cattle stampeded.

At first, it was as though they were going for a walk. Then it was faster; in seconds, they were moving directly at us, the chuck wagon, and the horse line. The cowboy who was to release the horse line was frozen in place. I was closest to him, so I turned my horse and rode to him, yelling all the way. This woke him up, and he took off.

The far end of the line was in a slip knot, so all he had to do was ride away with his end of the line tied off on his saddle horn. It would pull through the rings to which each horse had been tied so they were all freed quickly. That cowboy took off. I didn't see him again until daylight. He probably was the smartest one there.

As I turned back towards the other cowhands, I noticed that the cameraman was still on the job with his driver. Things were now fluid. The foreman and other two cowhands were riding towards me, followed closely by four hundred scared cattle.

The cattle were splitting us up; the two cowhands were forced to veer to the left, and the foreman, camera truck, and I to the right. The cattle were coming right up the middle. They did so, absolutely destroying the chuckwagon in the process. It tipped over, and then when the main body of cattle hit, it seemed to explode into pieces. There were no flames. It was smashed to smithereens. The foreman had come abreast of me when his horse found a prairie dog hole. He was thrown headfirst over the neck of the horse, which went down hard.

Without thinking, I reined my horse in and rode back towards the charging herd. I pulled the six-gun and fired above the cattle, hoping it would at least turn them aside. You would think even a panicked cow would hesitate to charge into something shooting flame.

Wrong. My horse was not thrilled but stopped as I sawed on the reins. The horse and I stood over the foreman as the cattle did veer enough that we were left standing. It seemed like it took a hundred years for those cows to pass us, but it was probably less than a minute.

Lee Sawyer, the foreman, had a broken arm. His horse was in a bad way. Its leg had multiple fractures, and the bone was poking through the skin. I did the only humane thing I could do. I hated pulling that trigger once more, but there was no other option.

About this time, the other two hands rode up. I noticed the camera truck was still there with all its lights on. Using my bandana and pieces of the shredded wagon, I made a crude splint and sling for Lee.

After that, I helped Lee into the back of the truck, He was starting to fall into shock. Using my blanket, we wrapped him, elevated his feet, and sent the truck back to the ranch house. There, the first aid team could treat him until they could get him to the doctor in Craig.

The cameraman wasn't thrilled about leaving me but followed orders.

"Now what, boss?" asked one of the remaining cowboys.

"What do cowboys do when the cattle get loose?" I asked.

"We round them up."

"Well, we need to get busy."

That's what we did until after daybreak. We decided to capture as many of the horses as we could. That way, we would have more riders to help us. By the time the first truck with real help, including Mr. Easterly, arrived, we had a dozen. Someone else went through the chuckwagon wreck, salvaging the saddles stored there overnight.

I was glad to catch a ride back to the ranch for breakfast and sleep. There would be no filming today. The cattle were scattered over five square miles. It would take days to round them up.

I ate pancakes for breakfast and went to bed. I did manage to remove my boots before I fell asleep. I woke up six hours later feeling better. After a shower, I was interested in coffee. Most of the crew was sitting around a campfire when I strolled up.

Chapter 17

I couldn't believe it when they all stood and started applauding!

"What's this for?" I started to ask but got cut off by Mr. Dodge the director and John Wayne.

Mr. Dodge told me, "Come look at this."

They took me into an old barn, which they had converted into a small theater for viewing the daily rushes. They played the film from the previous night.

The cameraman should win an award for how he caught all the action. The camera lights on the truck were powerful enough to cut through rain and dark to give an excellent sequence. He had it nailed from the moment I started riding towards the cowboy who was to let the horses loose until I had to put down the horse to take care of Lee Sawyer. I didn't know I was crying when I shot that horse until I saw the film.

"This film is gold, Rick. There will be no cutting or editing. It stands by itself."

"Unless, of course, you think we need another take," put in Mr. Wayne.

Without thinking, I replied, "Smartass."

As soon as I said it, I could see something horrible happening to me. Instead, Mr. Wayne laughed long and hard.

"I'm sorry, Mr. Wayne."

"Rick, something has to change right now. You will call me John from this day forward. You've earned it."

John never called me Ricky again.

The entire cast was called together.

Ron Dodge started, "You may have noticed part of the cast has decided to go for a walk."

It took me a moment to realize which cast members he was talking about.

"That has given rise to a problem and an opportunity. The opportunity is that with the footage of Rick Jackson last night, we will have a much stronger film.

"It will require a slight change in the storyline. This is where Sir Nick shows what he is made of. We would do that later when he and Big Jim face down the Regulators. We will still use that scene, but it won't be Sir Nick stepping up. It will be Sir Nick showing once again how strong he is.

"We will also have to do some scenes with Lee Sawyer to establish him in the movie. Mr. Easterly has agreed to his flying out to California. He won't be able to do real work like roping and branding for a while."

This gave a few chuckles.

"Now the problem is our work here is done, so we have to send you home starting today. Those who drove can leave anytime. The travel agency is working on seats for those who flew in commercial. Check with my secretary. She is set up in my office in the old barn."

There were cheers all around.

As I started to walk away, John caught up with me.

"I've chartered a small plane later today at the Craig airfield. Want a ride home?"

"I would appreciate that, Mr.... err...John."

I packed and spent the rest of the time with the Easterlies. I told him I was sorry about the stampede. That must have cost him all of his profit.

"Nah, Rick, this isn't my first movie involvement. I insisted on an insurance policy that covered a stampede; they can try to claim Act of God, but it is written that if they took off while under the studio's control, they had to pay."

"But it was your ranch hands there."

"I've got pictures of you giving orders and taking control."

"Ouch, will I get in trouble?"

"Think about that. A minor was left alone by the studio. No, you won't get in trouble, and I'm darn glad you were there for Lee's sake."

We shook hands, Mrs. Easterly and I embraced in a hug, and then I left for the airport with Mr. Wayne. I will think of him however I want!

The ride home was a little bumpy going over the Rockies but smooth the rest of the way. It was the way to travel. I definitely will be getting my pilot's license next year.

During the trip home, I updated Mr. Wayne on Detroit Faucet. John has been helpful to me, so I didn't want to blindside him. I didn't mention Anna Romanov, but he brought her participation up. She had talked to him.

That led to Mum Viscountess Margaret and my being the Honorable Richard Jackson in England. It seems David Niven told John part of her story but not the whole story.

"That would make quite a movie, Rick."

"I don't think she would be very receptive, but you never know."

It was still hard for me to think of my mum as a warrior.

It was late when I was dropped off at the Lockheed Air Terminal in Burbank. A taxi took me home in short order. I was glad to be back. There was no reading tonight. I couldn't get in that bed quickly enough.

Friday morning was wonderful. The weather was great. It felt good to do my exercises and then run. I met Dick Wyman as he was leaving his apartment. I updated him on my last two weeks as we ran around the high school track. He already knew about the stampede. There are no secrets in Hollywood.

When I went home to shower and change, my phone was ringing. It was a newspaper, but not one that I had been dealing with. I told them, "No comment," and quickly dialed my favorites. I was lucky and got through to both my contacts. They had me on their call today list, but I beat them. I gave them a synopsis of the location shoot, including the stampede and how it would affect the movie.

They both thanked me. As usual, I came up with a separate quote for each of them.

At the studio, I had a note to see Mr. Monroe as soon as I arrived. I only had to wait a few minutes and was shown into his office. He was different at work than at home. At his house, he was laid back and relaxed. At work, all business.

"I hear you had some excitement at the location."

"Yes, sir," I replied.

"You ever pull a stunt again, like riding that bull while working for me? I'll fire your ass. The liability is too much for us to handle. Yes, I know we should have better-qualified riders available. That is someone else's problem, and I'll talk to them later.

"Now that is out of the way, Rick. How are you? I understand you had nothing to do with that stampede and saved that guy. You weren't injured, were you?"

"No, sir," I replied.

"Good, Nina will be relieved. I had to force her to go to school today. She wanted to be here and make certain that you have all your body parts. Please stop by and see her after school, or my life will become hell."

"Yes, sir," I replied.

"Okay, get out of here. I've things to do."

"Yes, sir," and I got the heck out of there. I owed a thank you to Mr. Gordon. He taught me the hard way how to navigate trouble in the principal's office. It was a different office but the same concept.

On the set, we spent the morning doing lighting and sound checks. Boring but necessary was how it had been put to me. I agreed with the boring part. After lunch in the commissary, we walked through and practiced our lines. We still had a couple of weeks to go, but it was getting to the end.

It was nice to get back to working out in the stunt area. Sammy and I worked with the swords for half an hour. I had learned all the normal moves. Now, it was the practice to keep them reflexive. Rod Bell and I spent time at the archery butts, and that was more practice. My sword work was much better, as expected.

It still aggravated me that I couldn't do better at archery. After my one hundred shots, my arms were starting to wobble when I drew the bow, so I knew it was time to do something else.

Lifting was relaxing. My muscles were nicely defined, any more, and I would look like a powerlifter. I didn't want that, and it would limit the type of parts I could get. Looking to be in first-class shape was my goal. Now, it was maintenance, just like the sword work.

I thought about it for a while and then went back to Sammy. I explained to him where I thought I was at with lifting and the sword. He agreed. We revised my workout schedule to lifting three times a week and sword work twice weekly. I would practice with the bow each weekday until I reached a plateau.

Don Palmer, my boxing coach, and I already agreed on a similar plan for boxing. I will be starting my unarmed combat training next Monday. I was looking forward to it. I hated the helpless feeling I had when those two guys jumped me.

I stopped by Mr. Palmer's office and reconfirmed Monday as the start of my boxing with other opponents and unarmed combat training, or UCT. Then I was free for the weekend.

Back at my apartment, I collected all my receipts to mail to Grimes Accounting in Ohio. I stored them in a file cabinet in separate hanging files. I kept them bundled in order and packed them into a large shoebox for shipping. I wonder if the Grimes family would get the joke.

On my way to Nina's, I went through a car wash as the Bird was looking dusty. When I pulled up to her gate, she must have been waiting because I was let in immediately. I swear she tried to give me a physical in the driveway. She started with an in-depth tongue probe while feeling most of my vital parts. Well, not the private parts, but she did run her hands all over me.

Next, the grilling began. Why did I get involved in such stupid activities as riding a bull and getting caught in a stampede? I have never claimed to understand women, but I knew my answer would be wrong. Not even the "yes, sir; no, sir" would work here.

I found that lowering my hands around her while conducting my probes cut the questions off. Finally, the sound of the gate opening to let Mr. Monroe in saved me from having to give any answers as to my lack of common sense and all-around general stupidity.

I don't think telling her it seemed to run on both sides of my family would be a good defense.

Mr. Monroe was his normal laid-back, at-home self. I wondered which was the act, work or home. Could he separate the two so thoroughly? Neat trick if he could. He was going out to dinner, so Nina and I decided to go to the Hamburger Hamlet.

We arrived at the most crowded time. There wasn't even a spot in the parking lot behind the restaurant. We had to park down the street and then walk back to the rear entrance. There was no front entrance on the street, which was strange.

There were no tables available, but Nina saw a couple she knew, and they allowed us to join their table. She introduced me to Ann and David. She was an English girl. He wasn't much taller than her but impressed the heck out of me. He had just enrolled at MIT. You don't get in there unless you are really smart. That was on my list of places I would like to go to college.

They were a fun couple, and we enjoyed our conversation.

After dinner, Nina and I went to a movie. *The Bridge on the River Kwai* was playing at a small theater, and we both had seen it before but thought we would enjoy it again. We did enjoy it in the back row of seats.

I took her home slightly before eleven to make her curfew. I was glad to get home myself; it was a tough week.

Chapter 18

Sunday, I did my routine exercises and then did something I hadn't done for a long time. I went to breakfast at the small diner. Then, I did nothing for the rest of the day.

When I woke up Monday, I thought it was good to be home. That was interesting. Was this apartment now home?

As John would say, "We're burning daylight." There was nothing I was going to fret about.

I performed my exercise routine, and I went for my run. Dick Wyman was already on the track.

"Hey, Dick, how's it going?"

"Pretty good, and you?" he responded.

"Just fine. I'm glad to be back and able to resume my routine."

"Yeah, location shots are fun, but getting back home is always good."

About that time, we were passed by what I thought of as a thundering herd. It was about twenty high school kids. They looked young, like freshmen. Loping along behind them was a man, obviously their coach.

"Good morning, Coach," I said as he started to pass.

He returned the greeting, adding, "I've seen you two run here in the morning before. We usually aren't out this early, but these slackers need the extra work. You guys don't seem to be that fast, but you do go some distance. What do you run, two or three miles?"

Dick answered, "Five miles every day."

Coach eyed me as he ran alongside us, "You're still in school, aren't you?"

"Yes, sir. I just completed the California exams for the ninth grade, so I'm out for the year."

"How did you manage that?"

It took a few minutes to give him a broad outline of who I was and what I had been doing. In the meantime, his team passed us twice. A couple of the guys made snide remarks about me not running fast. They were also careful not to include their coach in the remarks.

The coach asked me, "Feel like teaching a couple of smartasses a lesson?"

"I'm always up for some fun, Coach."

The next time the group came around, he snagged the two guys making the remarks.

"Since both of you are so much better than everyone else, I want you to show this guy how to run. He sets the pace, but you keep going until he drops."

"Sure, thing, Coach," the mouthier of the two replied.

It didn't work out as Mouthy planned. After three miles, he was lagging. After four, he was puking. The coach had kept the rest of the team in the stands as we ran by. Now he was out there explaining to them how their mouths shouldn't write checks their bodies couldn't cash. Furthermore, if two old guys like Dick and I could run them into the ground, then they were a pretty sad bunch.

As we were making our way home, Dick had to laugh, "How does it feel to be an old guy?"

"You know, most of those guys are older than me." I laughed in return.

Dick's comment, "Old men, huh," on the way home, was the single mention of the matter. I'm glad I wasn't the only one stung by that comment.

That was a fun way to start the day.

At the studio, it was serious work. We were getting close to the end of filming. All the major scenes had been shot. Now, it was redoing those that they weren't satisfied with. There were also a couple of revisions to the story. They had decided not to display that Sir Nick was killed in World War I. The story would be left wide open, but there wouldn't be a sequel unless the show were a raging hit.

There was a quick break for lunch, but we had to get back to work as quickly as possible. We were at it until six o'clock, so I had to cut my activities in the stunt area short. I went directly to the gym. Coach Palmer was waiting with a guy who was about six inches shorter than me and fifty pounds lighter. I thought this would be an easy sparring match.

The guy was as quick as a striking snake. I was covering up in no time. I brought it under control by using my longer reach to force him back. Once I could keep him at a distance, I started to work with him. I wasn't hurting him, but I was keeping him from hurting me! Coach called the fight at that point. He told me his objective of teaching me how to handle a quicker opponent was achieved.

I touched gloves with my sparring partner, Al Escobar, and thanked him in Spanish for his time. He gave me a shy grin and told me it was fun and that he would take me if it got to a real match.

I laughed and told him, "I don't doubt it."

The truth was, I didn't doubt it at all. Man, was he quick.

I also realized that Coach's method of teaching me how to handle different opponents was to throw me into the deep end. After that, as a warm-up, he battered and threw me around for a while in what he called hand-to-hand combat training. I think I would call it Rick bashing.

After that painful experience, I headed home, took a shower, and put on fresh clothes.

I didn't feel like making my dinner, so I decided to go to the Brown Derby. It was appropriately upscale enough that I could wear my new snap-brim hat. It looked like the one Dean Martin and Frank Sinatra wore. Looking at myself in the mirror, I felt sharp as a tack.

The restaurant wasn't crowded. I had placed my order when a group of eight arrived. Six of them were bodyguards, and the other two were Frank Sinatra and a woman. Mr. Sinatra looked around the restaurant, and his eyes seemed to stop on me. He signaled to a very attentive Mr. Cobb, who hurried to his side.

Mr. Cobb was waving his head yes to whatever the question was. Mr. Sinatra then talked to one of the bodyguards, who promptly headed for my table.

"Mr. Jackson, if possible, Mr. Sinatra would like a few minutes of your time."

Of course, I wasn't about to say no. I started to rise, but the bodyguard raised his hand in a gesture to stop me.

I realized that Mr. Sinatra was coming to me! What was going on?

Upon arriving, Mr. Sinatra held out his hand, and we shook.

"I only need a minute," he said, "I would've had to call you to arrange a meeting. This works nicely. A friend of mine, Mr. Salvatore Lucania, asked to give you a message to pass on to your mother."

Being bewildered, I raised a single eyebrow. He gave me a sharp look but continued. "Boots Moran had loose lips. What he did wasn't authorized, and we do not quarrel with Viscountess Jackson or her employers. Would you please pass that on from Mr. Lucania?"

"Yes, sir," I replied.

"Thank you. I appreciate the respect from youngsters. By the way, that is a nice hat," pointing at my hat sitting on the chair next to me.

"Thank you, sir."

And that was the end of my conversation with Frank Sinatra. I would have to give Mum a call when I returned home.

It wasn't past eleven in Ohio, so I called. She gave a slight laugh when I passed the message. "Lucky was always the careful one."

"Who's Lucky?"

"He's no one you want to know. I met him in the war. He helped with some problems on our docks, similar to the ones in New York."

She wouldn't say anything beyond that. She did add a cryptic statement. "W, at the Circus, has sanctioned any actions, and our cousins have gone along with it.

"We love you, Rick. Good night."

I had no sooner hung up than the phone rang. It was my reporter friend from the *LA Examiner.*

"Ricky, what did Sinatra have to say tonight?"

I knew gossip made the rounds quickly, but this was ridiculous!

"He liked my hat," I replied.

"I know that. My source heard that much. What else?"

"He wanted to know if I was interested in performing a duet with him."

"You're kidding!"

"Would I kid you?"

"In a heartbeat. What did he say?"

"I'm sorry. It was a private message for the Viscountess."

"The Viscountess?" he inquired.

"My mum, haven't you heard?"

That opened the floodgates. Neither he nor anyone else in the American media knew about my mum. When I finished telling that story, Mr. Sinatra was forgotten.

"Will she let me interview her?"

"I'll call her for you, but I suspect she will want to first talk to George Weaver, a local reporter. He has been a friend of the family for a long time."

"Is he any good as a writer?"

"I think so."

"If you have his number, maybe he and I can do a story with a joint byline. That would be good for both of us. I could help him with the national questions, and he would add the local flavor."

I gave him George's number and hung up. Of course, that was just the beginning. The most fun was with the tabloid writer. He was ready to describe the affair Sinatra and Mum were having. I reminded him that her title, as a viscountess, was created for her actions in the war, and maybe he should tread lightly. When I shared why Mum was a viscountess, he backed off and asked me what he should write about.

I gave him the duet line as a joke, and to my surprise, he wanted to run with it. I had no problem with that but figured heck would freeze over before I would get a duet with Sinatra.

The phone rang again. It was Mr. Sinatra.

"Hey kid, have you been getting many calls?"

"Yes, I have two from reporters." I named them.

"What did you tell them?"

"I derailed the *Examiner* with Mum's story. That was about to break anyway. The tabloid wanted you two to have an affair. I reminded him of what Mum did to earn her title. That took care of that. I then told him that you had approached me about doing a duet with you."

That gave Mr. Sinatra a laugh, "I've listened to 'Rock and Roll Cowboy'. No, thank you."

"I understand; it was all I could think of on the spur of the moment."

"It's no problem, kid. I just don't want to have our stories conflict too much."

"That could be a problem."

"Thanks, Rick. We will keep you posted from this end."

After we said good night once more and hung up, I disconnected the phone. I tried to read but couldn't focus. I kept coming back to Mum and her connections. I had assumed her stories in the SOE and MI6 were in her past. Now, I wasn't sure. Was my Mum a female 007? What role did Dad play in all this?

The more I thought about it. I realized that she couldn't be an active agent. She was always there for us kids. Her recent trip to England was the first time I could remember her being away from home.

Clearly, the mob thought she had done Paul Grant in, and the British and American governments agreed and sanctioned it. She must have some serious credit with them. Saving the future queen's life wouldn't get her a free pass forever. What else had she been involved in?

Another interesting thing was the confirmation that Sinatra had contacts in the mob. He probably was only being used to pass a message, but that hinted that he was known and trusted to do so. I would have to be cautious there, although there probably would be no further contact between us.

Chapter 19

The next morning, I brought Dick Wyman up to date on the happenings as we ran. Considering we were running, we did well as we talked the whole way. Sinatra wowed him. Mum's story blew him away. He veered off the track and almost tripped when I told him I had the courtesy title of "The Honorable Richard Jackson."

He said, "You do realize the papers will shorten your name to something like HonRick when they write about you?"

"That will be better than the RickyJ they are now using."

"Lord only knows what they will call your mother."

"If I were them, I would be very careful about that."

"You're right. Some people you don't want to piss off."

When I arrived at the studio, the guard flagged me down with a message. Mr. Monroe would like to see me. This could get interesting.

It was interesting, but not in any way I thought.

He started with, "Rick, you know there is a media storm coming your family's way? If the studio can help in any way, please let us know. I have asked our publicity group how to use this to the film's advantage. You have had some publicity for your heroic actions, but not that of a media star. That is about to change."

"I appreciate that, sir. It is my parents' call if they want family help. Maybe you should talk to them. I'm okay with getting publicity for the film. I've not had that sort of experience, so I will need all the help you can give.

"As to my publicity, I want to come across as serious and responsible, not as a clown. Someone like Milton Berle can get away with outrageous dress and acts. That's not me or how I wish to be viewed."

"We will protect your image. That is exactly the sort of thing that needs to be decided quickly, what your image is going to be.

I checked, and there is no need for you on the set this morning. I would like you to get together with our publicity group. I would also recommend that you hire your own firm to represent you.

"Now, on to the important matter. My daughter has commanded me to invite you to dinner this evening. She wants all the inside information on Viscountess Jackson. I must say I'm curious about this myself."

"I would be delighted to have dinner, sir. One thing you may not have heard is that I was approached by Mr. Sinatra at dinner last night on a private matter. Reporters are trying to find out about that conversation."

Mr. Monroe was not president of Warner Brothers Studios by being slow.

"I trust that won't cause problems for your family?"

"No, just the opposite. I really can't get into it, but some people want to avoid problems with my family."

"Rick, you are the hardest working, most intelligent child star I have ever worked with, yet at the same time, you are giving me more heartburn and headaches than anyone else. One part is because I'm a father with a teenage daughter, and the other for the surprises that keep coming up around you.

"Next thing I'll learn, you're an adopted member of the Apache, and they're after me."

I remember my dad telling me there are times you have to act and times when you can think things through. This was not a time that I had to act, so I kept my mouth shut.

I met with the studio publicity team, headed by Jack Evans. I quickly discovered they weren't on the same page as Mr. Monroe. They could care less about my image. They wanted the most mileage for the studio they could get. One even asked if we could get my godparents to come to the premier.

I told him I would call the queen later today. He didn't even recognize the sarcasm. I cut that meeting as short as I could. It still wasted a couple of hours. There was a message waiting for me when I came out of that meeting. Please call Mr. Sinatra.

I asked for the loan of an empty office and called Mr. Sinatra back immediately. His conversation was to the point.

"This is getting out of hand. Too many people heard bits of our conversation at the restaurant. I need to distract them. I laughed about doing a song with you. Now I think I'm stuck with it."

"Don't do me any favors."

"Hey, I'm sorry. I didn't mean to insult you. From what I hear, you are the first to admit your voice isn't really strong enough to sing professionally."

"That's true."

"Would you mind if I called your agent and tried to set up a deal for a duet as a B side on a forty-five? We'll play it straight. If we can come to terms, we do the song. If not, we're covered either way. What do you say?"

"Call him. We can handle this."

We disconnected, and I sat in the office for a while thinking. I had just told one of the stars of the entertainment world, who had some sort of connection with the mob that "we can handle this." Am I insane?

Some of the books about navy warfare that I had read talked about damage control. I needed damage control badly. I'm in over my head.

I needed help now. Who could and would help? Who were my natural allies? I found a yellow legal pad and a ballpoint pen inside the desk's center drawer. First was my parents, then John Baxter my agent, and then Mr. Spiller my entertainment lawyer.

After that, there was the reporter from the *LA Examiner*, the stringer for *Variety,* and the tabloid reporter. They were allies of convenience, and it was their convenience, not mine. Maybe I should classify them as tools.

I had people such as Mr. Wayne and Miss Romanov, who I considered friendly, but there wasn't any reason to drag them into this. As I thought about it, I decided it was time to call Mr. Baxter. He took my call immediately, which was a good sign. I had been told stories about how you knew you were done in Hollywood when your agent wouldn't accept your calls.

"Richard, what the heck have you been up to? I've been getting calls all morning. What is happening between you and Sinatra?"

"That's why I'm calling you; he or someone from his staff will be contacting you about us singing a duet together."

"I thought you told me that you weren't interested in a singing career."

"I'm not. This is to be a one-time deal. I can't go into all the details, but Mr. Sinatra wants the negotiations to be public knowledge but hopes they don't go anywhere."

"So, do you want the deal?"

"I cannot lose by doing a record with Frank Sinatra, no matter the finances, even if it is only a B side on a forty-five. So, push them a little to get the best deal possible, but in the end, make the deal."

"Okay, you're the boss, and I think you are reading it correctly."

"There will be rumors about an additional conversation between Mr. Sinatra and myself at the Brown Derby. That was very private and involved my family. I want to stonewall anyone and everyone on that. You know nothing and have no comment."

"Well, that part is easy. I know nothing, so I couldn't possibly comment."

"I like that, 'I know nothing.' That would be a good line somewhere. Something else I need is a publicist. Can you recommend anyone?"

"I can. There is a lady whose only client just died. She is incredibly good. Considering what a slime bag he was, she kept his image positive and the bad news to a minimum."

"Who is that? And who was her client?"

"That's Susan Wallace, and her client was Paul Grant."

"You're kidding. Why would I want anything to do with her!"

"Because she is capable, and I have known her since she was a kid. She is a good woman who thought she had her big break. It looks like it might break her. I introduced her to Grant, so I feel guilty."

"So, you are willing to vouch for her on a personal basis?"

"Yes, her parents have been friends of ours for a long time. I watched Suzie grow up. I can guarantee that she was not part of Paul Grant's problems."

"I hope I don't regret this but based on your recommendation, I will talk to her."

"You won't be sorry, Rick, and you probably can get her services cheaply right now."

"Mr. Baxter, you of all people should know that is not how I or my family conduct business. Whatever she was making with Grant, I will match. If he was underpaying, I would give her an increase. Would you please contact her for me and arrange a meeting? Also, please determine what she should make based on her experience, training, and education."

"Yes, I will, and I forgot who I was speaking to. Please accept my apology."

"Accepted," I replied.

I wasn't happy about his initial response, but only one fight at a time. We exchanged a few more pleasantries and disconnected.

I next called home. Mum answered the phone. I brought her up to date on everything. She agreed that it was time I hired a publicist. She had reservations about Susan Wallace based on her previous employer. However, she conceded that hiring Susan, if she were suitable, could be a good publicity move in its own right.

We then talked about buying a house in California. Mum still thought it was the right thing to do.

Property values appeared to be heading up nationwide and would be doing so for some years. Dad's research in the business showed no downside currently, especially in expensive areas like Hollywood. She told me also to consider a house on the ocean. Their prices would be skyrocketing.

I asked her if she had any idea of the price ranges I should seek. She didn't but would discuss it with my father. They would probably end up talking to a realtor based out here in California.

"Mum, what do you mean by currently? Are things likely to change?"

"I've learned that things change, and seldom for the better. I've no reason to see a danger in the immediate future, other than there has always been the chance of danger in my future and those I love ever since I started my path in life."

"Mum, that sounds like there is a lot that you haven't told me. Will you ever?"

"Someday, Rick. Now is not the time. I will tell you everything you need to know when you need it."

She let me know that she had a call from the studio offering their services in preparing statements. She also was interviewing with George Weaver later in the day, with some questions provided by the reporter from the *LA Examiner*. She told me George had been thrilled with the idea of having his name on a national byline.

"Mum, one last question; do you have a 00 number from MI6?"

She started laughing. "Rick. You've been reading too much of Ian Fleming's nonsense. There were never 00 numbers!"

"Oh."

We exchanged I love you as we were hanging up. Right at the last second, I heard in almost a whisper, "We're Omega agents."

O... Kay. I probably don't have a need to know, and maybe I have a need to not know.

Chapter 20

Then, to keep my lines of communication open with the reporters I knew, I called each of them about the possibility of me singing with Sinatra.

With all those calls done, it was lunchtime. I had enchiladas at the commissary. I was developing a taste for Mexican dishes with an American twist. Still, nothing beats a Coca-Cola to wash it all down, well, maybe a Royal Crown Cola on occasion. If you were eating a Moon Pie, RC Cola was the only way to go.

I wandered over to the set, but they did not need me, so I spent the afternoon working out in the stunt area. It felt good to be physically doing something. I felt like I had a mental overload. Sammy and I went at it with the swords.

Afterward, he told me I was good enough for an actual fight. If they ever do Elizabethan reenactments, I'd have it nailed. That was an opportunity to tell him about the 6th OVI, of which I was a very new and junior member. He was interested.

Sammy told me, "We are always looking for people who know about a specific period to act as experts to keep us semi-straight."

I had to laugh at the semi-straight. The movie had me in a gunfight in the street with a member of The Hole in the Wall Gang. There was never a recorded gunfight in the Old West. There were plenty of ambushes and bushwhacking but no so-called showdowns on Main Street.

I performed my one hundred shots with my longbow, then lifted weights.

Lifting weights afterward actually cooled me off. It also got me ready to box. Today's fight was with a big heavy hitter. I mean huge. He was taller than me and heavier. He would be a super heavyweight. If he touched me, I was done.

So, I didn't let him touch me. It was more like a Fred Astaire dance than a boxing match. I backpedaled as much as possible while he tried to corner me so he could whale the tar out of me.

After three rounds in which he hadn't caught me, and I hadn't hit him, Coach made me plant my feet and go at it. I took hits, heavy hits, but stayed up. I managed to work the guy's stomach over pretty well, but not enough. After a round of that, Coach called it.

"Today's lesson was to take a punch and keep going. Class dismissed."

The big guy didn't say a word; he just got out of the ring and left before I could thank him. Nice guy! I mentioned that to Coach.

"He was paid pretty well for doing this. He just recently lost a major and is having a hard time adjusting to the fact that his professional boxing days are over. In his hay day, he would've killed you."

"Thanks for the vote of confidence, Coach; I think."

In UCT, starting with one defensive move, you set your opponent up for a certain offensive move. If he used a particular defensive move against your offense, you had another move to make.

Coach said, "You make moves and countermoves until one of you can't move."

I wondered if Mum could do this stuff.

Later, I headed home, showered, and changed clothes for dinner at the Monroe's. My California informal dress was the right choice. The only people present were Mr. Monroe and Nina, who dressed similarly to me.

I wore my new snap-brim hat. Mr. Monroe admired it and wanted to know if that was the one Sinatra liked. That opened the conversation. Between them, I felt like I was being interrogated. I didn't tell them Mr. Sinatra's real message or what Mum had related to me. Other than that, I gave them the whole Viscountess Jackson story.

Since confession is good for the soul, I told them about the possible record with Mr. Sinatra. Mr. Monroe knew most of this, but Nina hadn't heard it in school yet. She could hardly wait for tomorrow because she would have all the hot gossip.

Hollywood High had the children of both actors and those actors' house servants. If they didn't know about it, no one did.

Nina walked me to my car later, and we necked a little. Her heart didn't seem to be in it. I asked her what was wrong. She proceeded to tell me that today, her plans to spend the summer in France with her mother and go to a private Swiss school next year were finalized.

I hugged her tightly but didn't have much to say. It wouldn't happen for a while. I also remembered a comment Mr. Monroe had made earlier in the day about being the father of a teenage daughter. Whenever I decided I liked a girl, she would move away. Would she move away if I didn't like a girl but pretended I did?

It wasn't like this had been a great romance. We liked each other and had fun exploring sexual possibilities without doing anything. We had never used terms like love or steady or forever.

On the way home, I thought about it. I realized that things were working out okay. We were friends, and things might have been different if we had met in the future. In the meantime, we had a good relationship. I was certainly more comfortable around girls than at the beginning of the year.

At the studio, there was a message at the gate. The guard, Bill, who I was getting to know pretty well, flagged me down and handed me a pink "While You Were Out" slip. The note was to call Mr. Baxter before lunch. I made the call before going to the set. He wanted to know if bringing Susan Wallace for lunch today at the commissary was okay. It was all right with me. If nothing else, it would be a cheap date since he would bill me for lunch.

After makeup and costuming, I did several scenes with Lee, the ranch foreman, and Ellen, his daughter, in *Sir Nick*. They were all inside, with no action, just talk, so I ended up clean, which was a pleasant change.

The morning went quickly. One funny event happened. Raul Rodrigues, my prop man friend, stopped by while I was watching the scenery being changed. We talked for a while.

When we were almost done, he said, "Rick, do you know you've been talking in Spanish with a British accent?"

That was a first. I didn't even know I could do that. Raul and I goofed around for a few minutes, and he swore I could speak Spanish with a Spanish, American, or English accent at will. That might come in handy someday.

At lunch in the commissary, I met Susan Wallace. John Baxter was there to introduce us. He handed me a slip of paper with two numbers on it. One was what she should be making, the other what she earned with Paul Grant. He was a slime bucket in more ways than one.

Susan was dressed professionally in a skirt and jacket. She didn't wear a hat and gloves, but you could tell she would be comfortable in them. She was in her mid-twenties and was petite.

She quickly clarified that this session had two portions: me interviewing her for a job and her deciding if she would work for me! Based on her recent experience, that seemed fair, so I went with the flow.

"What would you like to know about me, Susan?"

"What have you been convicted of?"

Well, that was straight to the point.

"Nothing."

"Okay, what arrests, and how did you get off?"

"There have been no arrests, so there has been no need to get off anything."

"Then what trouble have you gotten into?"

Man, she is like a bulldog.

"I had a lot of detention days for trying to move Mr. Watkins's desk from his classroom to the stage in the auditorium. It did get commuted to cleaning up the school grounds because there wasn't enough time to serve the detention before I came out here."

"You mean to tell me that high school detention is the worst that ever happened to you?"

"Yes, ma'am."

My fingers were crossed because I wasn't about to tell her how the Justice Department had sent me a warning letter about discharging a firearm on federal property. If that story ever got out, more than my image would be in trouble.

"How much alcohol do you consume, and what drugs do you use?"

"None of those ever." This statement got a look of disbelief.

"What about women, err, girl trouble?"

"No girl trouble, only one girlfriend at a time, and I haven't figured out how to get to second base yet."

I thought she was going to choke on that one, she laughed so hard.

"I will be checking on all that."

"Fine by me," I replied, thinking this woman didn't hold back.

"That was the bad stuff. Now tell me about the good stuff."

"I'm an Eagle Scout with three lifesaving awards, and I'm an Honorary Texas Ranger. The Shawnee Indian tribe considers me a friend. I hold patents for inventions, an adjustable showerhead, and a portable hairdryer. I'm also a 6th Ohio Volunteer Infantry member, a Civil War re-enactment group.

"I have made one record and may be in line to make another. As you probably know, I've been in several movies. I'm working on *Sir Nicklaus*, the second lead behind John Wayne. I have a signed contract for a new movie starting later this month, working title, *Bandits of Sherwood.*

"My godmother is Queen Elizabeth II of England, and my godfather is President Eisenhower. My mother is Viscountess Jackson, and I have the courtesy title of The Honorable. I get along with my brothers and sister."

Susan responded, "I looked you up and talked to a few people before coming here. They told me most of what you have said. That is a pretty impressive resume for a fifteen-year-old. The only thing no one mentioned was the Shawnee Indian bit. What's that about?"

"I performed a service for the Shawnee, and they gave me an award. I'm not at liberty to say what that service was. They may tell you; I am honor-bound not to."

From the look on Susan's face when I said this, I had just done something to her worldview.

"Are you telling me that you will let your honor stop you from gaining favorable publicity?"

"Yes, I am," I replied curtly.

"I'm not used to that being a consideration," she replied softly.

"Is that a problem?" I inquired.

"No, it is the exact opposite. After my last client, it is a refreshing outlook. Several times, I felt like taking a shower and scrubbing with steel wool after issuing a press release. It makes my decision easy. If all you say is true, and I will check it out, I would like to work for you if possible."

"Susan, I'm willing to give you a chance for the same reasons. How much do you expect to make now that the hard part is done?"

She replied with a number that was more than she had made with Paul Grant but less than the industry standard. At the time, ten thousand dollars a year was an extremely good salary.

A good publicist would make fifteen thousand. Grant had been paying her eight. Not bad money, but not what the trade paid. She asked for twelve. I shook my head and countered with sixteen thousand plus expenses.

"You will also be on our corporate healthcare plan."

Sometimes having money is fun. This was one of those times. The look on her face was priceless.

"There is a catch."

The look of joy on her face closed down immediately.

"The catch is you will be doing publicity for all my companies, not only Jackson Entertainment.

She cautiously asked, "What companies?"

"Jackson Productions, Jackson Home Products, and Jackson Personal Products are all fully owned subsidiaries of Jackson Holdings." I went on to explain the hairdryer and adjustable showerhead.

"What would you want me to do with those companies? Since they are headquartered in this Bellefontaine, Ohio, would I have to move there?"

"No, you wouldn't have to move to Bellefontaine."

It was almost comic to see her relief. I guess to a Californian, small-town Ohio would be similar to Siberia.

"Let me start over as to what I want you to do. I need someone to manage my public image positively. My goal is not to be a world-class actor or entertainer. Those are things that have happened to me, but that isn't who I am or who I want to be.

"I'm not certain what I want to do with my life, but I know that whatever it is will require influence and money. Right now, I'm thinking of a company to mine the asteroid belt."

It's a shame there isn't a way to have cameras running all the time. The look on her face was priceless when I mentioned mining the asteroid belt.

"I'm fifteen years old, so my goals may change. There is about a one hundred percent chance they will change. My point is that whatever I end up doing, I won't be able to accomplish it without a positive public image. It may even get to the point of wanting no image. I just don't know. To achieve that, you would have to be involved in, or at least aware of, all my activities."

"Mr. Jackson, I think I'm going to enjoy working with you."

"Great. Since I know everything I've told you is true, I'm going to have my lawyer draw up a contract. It will have no surprises, but still, have your attorney review it."

"I've learned that lesson the hard way." We shook hands, and I thought that was a well-spent lunch.

Back at the set, they told me they were going to have to redo the throwing me in the water trough scenes. This became a running joke. I did manage to work in a phone call to Mr. Spiller, the entertainment lawyer, and had him start a contract for Susan Wallace as head publicist of Jackson Holdings. The title was his suggestion. He had experience in this area and knew what worked.

I had to explain to him what my goals in life were, or weren't, as the case may be, so he could understand what responsibilities she would have. He found it intriguing because he hadn't run into anyone in the entertainment business with my attitude.

I think he was kidding on the square when he said, "Since you aren't looking for stardom, you will probably find it."

Today was Ellen's turn to be tongue-tied on the set. It required us nine takes for one scene. She misspoke in the first three. I broke up laughing in the fourth as I waited for her to make an error. She whacked me hard for that. During five through seven, she was tongue-tied again. The eighth worked well, but the director wanted at least one more take as a safety. The last one was probably the best try of the day.

After that, Ron Dodge called the day a wrap. He had taken all he could stand today. I went over to the stunt area and went through my normal routine. Today there was no swordwork. All the time was spent on archery.

Rod Bell was there and taught me how to drop an arrow on a target. Rather than a flat trajectory, it was an arc. That way, the arrow would fall from the overhead. It is just a matter of figuring out the correct angle for the distance involved. For some reason, this came easier to me than hitting the bull's eye with a flat shot. Not that I was that great, but I could hit a ten-foot square laid out in a field two hundred yards long.

Not enough to hit people, but I could scare the rabbits.

Boxing today was against a dancer; at least, he had his footwork down. He didn't have a hard punch, but I had a hard time hitting him. I finally figured out I had to barrel in and push him into a corner. Once I did that, Mr. Palmer called it a bout with the lesson learned.

I felt like having a good burger for dinner, so I drove over to the Apple Pan. It wasn't much to look at, but the burgers were fantastic. I loved the steak burger and the relish they used. The slice of apple pie and vanilla ice cream didn't hurt things at all. I found a single seat at the U-shaped counter when I got there. It was neat to see your burger cooked in front of you.

I recognized the gentleman next to me, Mr. Gregory Peck, but kept to myself.

I was surprised when he turned to me and asked, "Are you, Richard Jackson?"

"Yes, sir, I am."

He extended his hand, and we shook. He told me that I had been pointed out to him at the Brown Derby. He was there at the same time as Frank Sinatra. He was very polite and didn't ask me what Mr. Sinatra wanted with me.

Mr. Peck worked for Twentieth Century Fox and was currently filming a movie, *The Bravados*. He told me a little about it. Mr. Peck thought it had a lot of good points, but something was missing. He turned the conversation to me.

After asking several probing questions about my future in the movies and acting in general, he advised me to become involved with a stage play. He thought that was where you learned the craft. He recommended that I attend tryouts at the La Jolla Playhouse in San Diego. I told him I would consider it. All in all, we had a pleasant conversation.

When I returned home, I called Nina. The first words out of her mouth were, "I hate you!"

Wow!

"Why do you hate me?"

"Because you are done with this stupid ninth grade, and I have this history exam tomorrow, and I'm not ready for it!"

Not being stupid, I agreed I was hate-able for not having to face a history exam, and that it was probably my fault that she wasn't ready. This started her laughing. Once she settled down, she admitted that she had been putting off her studies. We kept the conversation brief so that she could prepare for tomorrow's test.

I elected to spend the evening reading my economics textbook. A radio station had a show featuring Paul Anka's songs, so I stayed with it. Supply and demand curves mixed funny with "All of a Sudden My Heart Sings", then there are the thoughts raised by elasticity and "Diana", a final touch was oligopolies with "You are my Destiny".

I'm not sure how much I absorbed, but it was a fun evening.

Chapter 21

Thursday was a regular day: up and exercise, run with Dick, shower, shave, etc. Bill, the gate guard at the studio, just waved as I drove onto the studio lot. Makeup and costuming didn't take long, although they did trim my hair. My hair needed not to grow an inch from the beginning of a scene to the end.

Well, it was important to them that the movie was consistent. I thought it would be cool to go from right-handed in one scene to left-handed in the next. Maybe we could have a hunchback and move his hump from side to side. Funny to think about, but it would never be done. The censors would let it through, but no one liked things that crude unless they were teenage boys.

The only place we could get stuff that good was *Mad Magazine*. I seldom missed an issue since I discovered it last year. Recently, the thought had occurred to me that one way I would know I was a success was if they picked on me.

Everyone was serious about work today. It was getting near the end, and everyone was ready to wrap it up. Side conversations were about the next job, the lack of a next job, and who might be hiring. Since my next role was already signed, I stayed out of those conversations. I didn't have enough influence to get anyone a job, and I didn't want to rub mine in.

At lunchtime, a runner hunted me up. There was a message from Mr. Baxter waiting for me up front. I finished my tacos and strolled up to the front office. The message was to call him, so I took a chance that he might be in at lunchtime.

He wasn't, but a secretary gave me a number for him. It was at an upscale restaurant. They asked me to hold when I told them who I was calling for. In a few minutes, Mr. Baxter picked up the phone. I apologized for making him get up from his lunch. He told me not to worry. They had brought the phone to his table.

That impressed me. I hadn't ever heard of such a thing. That was so cool, not having to get up for a phone call! He was a little cryptic while speaking in public. "The guy with the blue eyes has made an offer. I took what you told me seriously. They opened with a take or leave it, so I took it.

"It isn't a good deal. It works out to a penny a sale. It is going to be on an album and the B side of a forty-five. You will get ten thousand dollars if the album goes gold by selling a million copies. No way is the album going gold, the same for the forty-five. The song is upbeat and bouncy, like what he did in 'High Hopes'.

"It will be called 'Brother'. You're the younger, of course. He's trying to share his mistakes with you, so you won't repeat them, but you are determined to make your own. They sent over by messenger a copy of the lyrics. It is a cute song, but they won't push it.

"Since the *Twenty-One* scandal, people have been shy about how they push their products. Word is the government is going to step in. Payola is going to take a big hit."

"Mr. Baxter, remember the object of this exercise is to build my credentials, not necessarily make money, though that would be nice."

"Let's hope for both. In the meantime, they want to do this fast. Sinatra has an album almost completed and wants to jam this in. They have arranged for a music voice coach to work with you on Saturday to teach you the song. The contract also specifies if they deem your voice is not up to the song, it is a no-go."

"When is the recording being done?"

"Sunday, at Capitol," Mr. Baxter told me.

"Yikes, they don't want to do this, do they?"

"I've no idea what is going on here. I do know that they've already put the word out. You are signed with Sinatra.

"Rick, to change the subject, Susan is thrilled with her interview. She wants to check a few things, but I'm certain she is going to take the job. I appreciate your giving her a chance. She is a good kid who got started with the wrong guy."

"I think she will do a good job for me. Don't tell her, but I'm seriously considering opening an office out here for Jackson Holdings. It looks like I will be in California for the foreseeable future."

"I'll keep it quiet. Have you started looking for an office yet?"

"No, sir, I haven't. I'm more concerned about buying a house."

"What are you thinking of?"

When I was done describing what I would be looking for, he sighed and told me, "You won't be able to afford something like that. I know you are making serious money in the movies, but a house like that could cost half a million dollars."

"Oh, that is a relief. I thought they would go for a million."

That gave Mr. Baxter pause.

"You could look at a house that cost a million dollars?"

"Yes, sir. The movies aren't my main source of income. My inventions are."

Now, Mr. Baxter knew about my inventions but had never put it together that it would be serious money.

I continued, "I will be paying cash for the house. Is there any realtor you would recommend?"

"Rick, I haven't had any reason to look into the price range you are talking about. You are friends with Sam Monroe. Ask him. I would say John Wayne, but he lives down south near Newport."

"Well, I'm more friends with Nina than Mr. Monroe, but I will ask. Thanks."

Life seems to get more complicated all the time.

The day's shooting ran late, so I only practiced archery, boxing, and hand-to-hand combat. Those still took the better part of two hours, so it was past seven when I returned to my apartment.

I turned the radio on to my favorite station, one of the high-powered ones out of Mexico, and read more on economics. For some reason, "Come Softly to Me" by Fleetwood doesn't mix well with aggregate market disequilibrium. I couldn't think of a song that would, maybe "Tom Dooley".

This evening was not as fun as last night, but I was determined to figure this out. I wondered if I could audit a course or at least write down points I didn't understand and get someone to clarify. I needed these basic ideas if I was going to make a mark on the world.

Before falling asleep, I reviewed my upcoming week. Next week, we will finish filming the movie. That was on Friday, April 3rd, which would put April Fool's Day on Wednesday. I wondered what that would bring. I had no plans of my own but suspected I would have to watch out for Mr. Wayne. He still owed me one.

Then I had to fly to Columbus on Saturday to play golf with President Eisenhower on Sunday, as had been arranged long ago. It was only last year, but it seemed like a lifetime ago. Then back to LA for an intense week of hand-to-hand combat instruction. Then start *Bandits of Sherwood*.

In the morning, Bill the gate guard instructed me to stop at the front office for a message. It was from a voice coach giving me the time and place on Saturday for me to practice the song that I was doing with Sinatra. There were also instructions for Sunday's recording session.

Makeup and costuming were getting to be old hat for me, something to be done, no big deal. It wasn't like a horror flick where it took hours. Two scenes had to be reworked in the morning. The afternoon had one more scene to be redone, and that was it. I had plenty of time in the stunt area.

After a rousing swordfight with Sammy, it was on to weightlifting. I was concentrating on maintaining body definition rather than bulking up. I didn't want to look like Charles Atlas.

Rod Bell had me work more on arced shots. The ten-foot square seemed to be my accuracy, but I was getting better at judging the angle. The three-foot-long arrows would dig into the ground a foot and a half with a field point. I wondered what a war point with the wicked barbs would do.

Boxing was with a left-handed short guy built like a barrel. Once I understood how he was going to lead, he wasn't much of a problem. He didn't move much. However, I was in trouble if he caught me in a corner. I didn't let him catch me, and after three rounds, Coach called it.

I think Coach was concerned. I was getting too big for my britches as he tossed me around in hand-to-hand combat.

Maybe I shouldn't have said, "Catch me if you can," to my opponent.

At Nina's, I asked her dad about real estate agents. He was surprised that I hadn't gone to my studio liaison for help. I told him that it never occurred to me, as the guy didn't seem interested in anything involving me. He told me to ask my liaison next week for help.

Later, Nina and I made a trip to the Hamburger Hamlet. The usual suspects were there. Several people approached me and told me it was cool that I was going to sing with Sinatra. Word gets around Hollywood High quickly.

Nina and I went to the parking spot up on the hillside. We just talked about her going to France for the summer and then to Switzerland for school. I asked her if her parents were concerned about our relationship.

"No, Rick. This was planned long before I met you. I didn't tell you because you may have decided not to waste your time on me."

Of course, I had to assure her she wasn't a waste of time. That led to necking. I was getting good at that. At least, I thought so. I tried to move things along, but Nina gently pushed my hand away, so I let it go. We were there for less than an hour, so we missed the cop's drive-through.

I dropped her off at her house and returned home for the evening. I thought about cruising around, but to what point?

Chapter 22

Saturday, after my morning rituals, I went to the music coach's studio. It was all business. He had me run through it once. To give him credit, he almost hid his shudder.

"Mr. Jackson, you have a real problem with breath control. You try to force out words powerfully, and in doing so, you run out of breath, which in turn causes you to be offbeat. You understand; it sounds terrible."

"What can I do?"

"First, don't try to sing loudly. Try to sing with the music."

He had me sing through the song twice. Since it was a duet, Sinatra would do a stanza; I would do my part; then we would do the chorus together. I only did my parts of the song and the chorus for practice.

When I toned things down, they did get better. Even I could notice the difference. The music coach had been accompanying me on a piano very softly. He now put on a disk that had the instrument parts recorded.

It was easier to sing to this. I was learning the words of the song as we went. The more I knew the words and concentrated on staying with the instruments, the better it got. We did this for an hour, then took a half-hour break. During the break, the coach taught me breathing exercises, which he said would strengthen my voice.

This went on most of the day, never enough to strain my voice.

At four o'clock, he called it. "Mr. Jackson, you will do. If you concentrate on keeping in time with the instruments, keeping it soft, they can enhance your voice.

"In a recording studio, they can build your voice up. Don't appear in a nightclub. I don't think your voice will ever be strong enough for that. And for God's sake, man, never, ever, and I mean never, agree to do the "Star-Spangled Banner" at any event. You don't have the power or the range."

"What do you really think?" I asked him.

This gave the laugh I was hoping for. We shook hands, and I headed out. Today I cruised down the coast, and after dinner in that old hotel in Laguna Beach, I headed home.

The next morning, I did my usual workout and then headed to the recording studio. To my surprise, Mr. Sinatra wasn't there. I asked about him, and I was told they would just overlay my voice with his. They let me do a couple of practice run-throughs, then five times with the recording equipment on. I worked at keeping my voice soft and staying on time with the music.

At the end of five trials, the guy responsible told me, "We have enough to work with. You aren't as bad as I was told. This might work out okay."

Now that is some vote of confidence.

I spent the rest of the day cruising around Hollywood Hills, getting to know the general area. It would be nice to have an idea of locations before starting my house hunt.

That night I read about spider puppies. It would make life a lot easier to have an eidetic memory. I'm not sure Eldreth was a great loss. It was a fun read.

Monday started fast and kept going. My phone was ringing when I returned after my run. While it was early for me, it was mid-morning in Ohio. Mr. Grimes, Jr. wanted me to know they had some second thoughts about what insurance I would need. They were so concerned they called State Granger's home office.

They were glad they had. My account was now going to be handled by a risk-management specialist out of the home office. Grimes would still receive part of the premiums but considerably less.

Mr. Grimes told me, "Normally, we would be upset about losing the money, but in your case, it is for the best. You are an actor; people want to sue you; they know you are wealthy. You are a business owner; people will want to sue your business because they know you are rich. You are an investor. People will want to sue you because you have money."

"Then there is the issue of a fifteen-year-old owning two Ford Thunderbirds on his parents' auto policy while living alone in California. As we went through everything, I could hear the guy start to hyperventilate on the phone."

"This doesn't sound good. Am I insurable?"

"Oh, for enough money, anything is insurable. It isn't that bad. Your cars will have to be registered under your company names. Each of your companies will have separate policies. You will have your liability set. It will be expensive, but you will be covered for everything from people tripping at your front door to a worker falling into the crucible while pouring the casting for one of your showerheads.

"The company will even try to get ahead by recommending warning labels. They are the coming thing in liability cases. Labels like, 'Don't use this hairdryer in the bathtub. Electrical shock may occur, which could result in death or serious injury.'"

"You're kidding me, aren't you? People wouldn't be that stupid, and a jury would throw them out."

"Rick, there have been several cases recently that have gotten the industry on edge. I'm saying we will be trying to help on all these issues.

"Another thing they want me to ask you to consider is emancipation."

"Emancipation?"

"You are financially self-sufficient and living away from your parents. It makes you a legal adult."

"You mean I could drink alcohol?—Not that I want to."

"No, that is specifically prohibited by law. If the law specifies an age, you are bound by the law, but you can have things in your name and sign binding contracts. It cuts both ways. It means your parents would not be legally responsible for you or your actions."

"I need to think about that and get some serious advice."

"That's a good approach. In the meantime, State Granger will put together policies for you and your businesses. Your parents will have to pay and sign for them at this time. The company thinks it would work out to everyone's advantage if you and your parents were completely separated from a legal point of view.

"Rick, if you give your permission, we will work with Eugene Burke to develop the best set of policies for each business setup. We will then present them to you for your approval."

"I will call Mr. Burke and tell him to share the information needed."

"Thank you, Rick. We will get this worked out."

After our farewells, I called Mr. Burke. He surprised me with his answer once I explained what was going on.

"Rick, I can't handle the complexity of what is required. I came to that conclusion this morning. I can do the filing to set up your companies, but I don't have the expertise regarding insurance needed and other details after that."

"I thought State Granger would tell you what insurance I need."

"Rick, I don't doubt they are an honest company, but how do you know? Common sense says multiple quotes. Each company will have to quote on the same package to see if they are equal. Will it be the right package? Whoever develops that package will have an inside track because they will slant it toward their strengths.

"Now, you tell me that State Granger has suggested emancipation. The problem with that is that you will have the power to sign anything they present. Would you rather face a boy's parents or the boy in a business deal? Remember, they don't know you.

"More importantly, they don't know your Mum."

"What do you mean? Never mind; anyway, I think it is alright if you tell the State Granger people my company set ups and what each one will be attempting. In the meantime, I'm going to talk to my parents."

Mr. Burke said, "Rick, that is a wise move."

Next, I called home; Mum and Dad were both there, so I updated them on my conversations. Their reaction was that Eugene Burke was looking out for my best interests. State Granger would probably provide the insurance required, but how could we tell it was the best deal for us and what we needed?

Out of the conversation came questions. Where was I going to live? If the movie business was temporary, and I would be moving home, my parents could sign for me if needed. There was no question about insurance. I needed it no matter where I lived. I needed more help than Eugene Burke could provide to ensure I had the right insurance.

It would probably be a legal firm in Columbus if I moved home. If I stayed in California, then an LA group. If I moved home, I wouldn't need emancipation; emancipation made sense if I stayed in California.

So, the deciding question was, would I be staying in the movie business, then becoming emancipated, buying a house in California, and retaining a law firm there? No movies meant moving home and retaining an Ohio firm.

Dad said it best, "Rick, moving on is what people do in life. We love you and want the best for you. You have proven that you can handle your own life, so think about what you want to do and do it. Remember, you are fifteen. In three years, you will be moving on anyway."

"Dad, that is true, but there is an option you haven't mentioned."

"What's that?"

"The whole family moves out here."

That was a showstopper. We finally agreed that decisions didn't have to be made right away, so we would sit on it for a while.

I did make a call to Mr. Spiller, the entertainment lawyer. I asked him to draw up a contract for Miss Susan Wallace as the publicist for Jackson Holdings. I gave him her particulars, our agreed-upon, and Eugene Burke's telephone number to obtain the Jackson Holdings data. He told me it would be ready by Wednesday.

I still managed to get into the studio on time. After makeup and costume, I headed for the set. We were doing a retake of my getting my marching orders to head to America after disgracing our family with Queen Victoria. I was so in character that I had the thought, "The old cow needs a man. Albert has been dead forever."

People around me wondered why I started laughing.

I didn't even try to explain.

We went to lunch late, electing to finish up the scene we were working on. The union agent on set was starting to tap his foot by the time we had finished, which was a distraction and forced another retake. That was the first time that I had seen tension on the set. Fortunately, we got through it.

Lunch was the usual. Today's crowd consisted of the extras for a movie set in the jungle. I must say that Hollywood loves its stereotypes. I was sitting next to such a group. Black men dressed in grass shirts, bones in their noses. They were debating where the Dalai Lama would go in very educated voices. He had disappeared in Tibet. The smart money seemed to bet on India.

This said as much about Hollywood as you needed to know. What we will do for fame and fortune.

The afternoon consisted of reading lines into recorders for dubbing later. Try conversing with someone who isn't even there and keep all the emotion where it belongs. Someone dispassionately reading the lines to which you are responding isn't inspiring. That session couldn't end soon enough.

The saying is, "This too shall pass." It passed, but it passed painfully slowly. You could never guess what part of the job I disliked the most.

After an eternity, the lines were read, and the assistant director said it was a wrap. He got the message that I was looking for something to wrap around his neck.

The stunt area was such a relief. I needed to move around. Sammy and I had a rousing sword fight. I felt like I knew how to use the sword. Weightlifting was calming after the adrenaline rush of the fight.

Archery was more of the long-range arced flights. I was doing fairly well at judging the arc needed. One ranging shot and I could usually hit the ten-foot square that was laid out one hundred and fifty yards away.

Boxing was against a guy whose arms must have been five feet long. Not really, but his reach had me dancing all over the place to avoid it. The solution was to move in, take some hits, and then knock the tar out of him. Coach called it after four rounds, saying, "Lesson learned."

Unarmed combat was a different story. I was still learning the moves. Every time I was doing one smoothly, Coach would introduce a response or variation. I spent time on the mat, slapping my hand to surrender. This was the preferable result. Flying through the air to land flat on your back sucks.

Dinner was In-N-Out.

That night, I read of the adventures of Dagny and Hank against an over-regulated society. In the end, I was so glad to find Galt.

Chapter 23

In the morning, I did my usual exercise sets and ran. The track coach wasn't there with his group, so I didn't have to feel like an old man. I did remind Dick that he was elderly. This resulted in his water bottle being poured on me. It felt good.

On the set, the tensions of yesterday had settled down, and we went through the scenes being reshot smoothly. I wonder if everything we had done before was a rehearsal for this. By now, we all were familiar with our parts and lines. It felt so natural going through things. I mean, for heaven's sake, off the set, I started with "Uncle Jim" when asking Mr. Wayne a question.

He laughed it off and then told me I could never accept a role as a serial killer if I were going to get into my part that deep. Now, that was a scary thought.

Lunch was with my faux African friends and World War I doughboys. Never a dull moment at lunch on the lot.

The afternoon was an eternity of voice dubs. I quit whining and just did them.

After half of infinity, I was released to the stunt lot. We skipped the sword today and spent all the time on archery. I enjoyed it, especially when I hit the target! I was getting better but was far from being competitive. At the end of the session, Rod Bell brought out a long case.

"Rick, you have advanced nicely, and since you have stuck to it, I would like to present the bow you will be using in *Bandits of Sherwood*."

I opened the case, and inside was a gorgeous yew English longbow. I knew this because a plaque inside the case stated, "This ninety-pound pull, yew-wood longbow was produced in the original style for use by Richard Jackson in *Bandits of Sherwood*."

There was a package of five reverse-twisted linen bowstrings. There was a new glove and arm protectors like I was used to. Rod also presented me with two bundles. There was a quiver in each one, with twenty-five field points and one with twenty-five wicked-looking hunting or war points.

I thanked him profusely. I had nowhere to keep them at the studio, so I took them home when I finished.

Weightlifting was a breeze. I was thinking about using my new bow.

Boxing was strange. My opponent was short, slow, and couldn't move around. I hated to hit him. He just wouldn't give up. I finally tore into him during the third round. "Lesson learned," said Coach.

"Coach, I don't understand this lesson."

"Simple, you will outclass some guys, but they are too dumb to know it. The only way to stop them is to beat them."

I looked over at the little guy who was still standing there. He winked at me. It takes all types, I guess.

As usual, it was a nice day, so I had the top down on the car. It was also the only way I could fit my new bow in the backseat of the T-Bird.

On my way back to my apartment, traffic came to a stop. I was about the twentieth car back in the holdup. I was stopped near a park. It wasn't much of a park. There were some swings in the front corner. There was a huge, wide-open space with the remains of a building in the center. The building had adobe walls but no roof. It was about thirty feet to each side. I couldn't see much over the seven-foot-tall walls, but I thought it was one large space inside.

Now that I was looking at what was there, I realized that police surrounded the whole lot. The lot was three hundred yards to each side. There must have been a hundred cops out there.

There was an empty sedan sitting near the building. Since traffic was going nowhere, I exited the car and approached the crowd on the sidewalk. I asked one of the men, "What's going on?"

"From what I have put together, five guys are holed up. A bank robbery went bad; they shot a guy who may be dead. They fled the scene and, for some reason, pulled over here and holed up inside. They are armed with rifles and handguns. The police are hesitant to charge their position because of the losses they will take."

There was a policeman on crowd control keeping everyone back. I approached him. "Officer, are there any hostages?"

"I don't know. I haven't heard that there are any."

"I may have a way to persuade those guys to come out."

"What's that?" he asked.

"Let me show you." I returned to my car and got the case with my longbow. I took it back and opened it for the officer.

You could see the wheels turn, "You can use this?"

"Good enough for this job. All I have to do is put arrows into their compound, and they will want to leave."

The officer turned and yelled, "Hey, Sergeant."

A slightly older man in uniform came over.

"Sarge, this guy says he can flush them out."

The police sergeant eyed me. "And how would you do this?"

I showed him the bow.

"I have arrows in my car."

"Get them and come with me."

Leaving the case with the police, I fetched my arrows, both quivers.

The sergeant led me over to a group of police gathered over the hood of a car. This was their command center. The man in charge was on a radio microphone extended from inside the cruiser.

He said, "Captain, we need a tank to dig them out.

"Yes, sir. I understand that it will take hours to get them here. I won't send my men in as it is; this isn't World War II.

"I know they might get away when it gets dark. We have already tried to position some cars around the field, and they are shooting their headlights out as fast as we can move the cars. I understand the mayor wants these men taken. Maybe he can come down and lead the charge himself.

"Sorry, sir. I will keep you posted."

The plainclothes officer signed off and turned to us.

"Lieutenant, I think we have our answer."

"What is it, Sergeant?"

The sergeant gestured, and I opened the case he returned to me.

"That would do the trick. Sergeant, please start shooting arrows into the compound."

That wasn't what I had in mind, but I just held out the case to the sergeant. He looked at it and then at me.

"How do you string it?"

I strung it for him. My initial irritation settled down. I knew how this would play out.

It went as I thought. The sergeant tried to hold the bow out straight and pull the string back. He couldn't pull it halfway back. The lieutenant signaled for a younger, bigger guy to try. He didn't do much better.

The lieutenant looked at me, "You can use this?"

"Yes, sir."

"Then please shoot into the compound."

"I have a question first."

"What?" came impatiently.

"Is there anyone but the bandits in there?"

"No, a couple of teenagers were necking, but they got out before they were trapped."

"These guys shot someone?"

"Yes, now shoot the damn bow."

"Not yet. I want some legal cover. I would hate to get sued by a bank robber for injuring him."

The lieutenant started to swell up but suddenly deflated.

"You are right. The courts are getting crazy. Raise your right hand."

Just like that, I was a sworn temporary Los Angeles Police Department member. I think my Rowland ancestor would be proud.

I didn't mess around. I bent the bow and let loose with a field point.

"Ranging shot," I explained.

It arced out one hundred yards to land just in front of the compound. I had the sergeant hold the quiver of war points for me. I quickly reached in and fired five arrows, one after the other.

An English longbowman, in practice, could shoot ten to twelve a minute. I think I got five off in a minute. They all soared up and landed inside the compound.

The result was immediate. The last one landed, and there was a blood-curdling scream.

Right after that, there were yells of, "We surrender."

The lieutenant used a bullhorn to tell them to come out, hands up, unarmed. They did. One of them had two feet of an arrow sticking out of his shoulder.

The cops grabbed and cuffed them. An ambulance was on standby, so they loaded the one with the arrow sticking out of him and hauled him away. I noticed there were a lot of pictures being taken. The police were working to keep people back.

One of the policemen went inside the compound. He yelled for the lieutenant. Once he was inside, the lieutenant signaled for me.

"Robin Hood, you can collect your arrows after we take pictures."

I wondered why he called me Robin Hood, and then I saw the arrows spread. Four of the war points were buried a foot into the ground, forming a rough square. In the center of that square was a splash of blood where my fifth arrow had landed. I didn't know what to say. I couldn't duplicate that in a million years. I ended up keeping my mouth shut.

The lieutenant took me aside.

"Thank you very much for your help. Now there is going to be a press conference. My captain and mayor are on the way. Can I count on you to try to make the department look good in this?"

"That is no problem, as nothing I saw would make you look bad."

"I was thinking about the men not being able to draw that monster bow of yours."

"It took me a lot of work to be able to handle the Monster, as you call it. We won't say anything about your men. I volunteered. You deputized me, and it worked."

"Thanks. By the way, what is your name again?"

I told him once more. He didn't recognize me for anything, so I informed him that I was an actor getting ready for a new Robin Hood-type movie. He thought that was neat as he had called me Robin Hood.

We stood around as the news media gathered. The mayor and police captain showed up. All the usual platitudes were expressed. I was introduced briefly as a citizen who volunteered to help. The mayor started to go on, but while the police and mayor didn't recognize me, the reporters did.

The headline that night was, "Robin Ricky Saves the Day—Again!"

After all the questions had been answered, the mayor took me aside and told me that there would be a special award from the city. The mayor was an expert politician and wanted to stay on the good side of Hollywood and its major donors.

I finally got back to my car and headed to the apartment, where my ringing phone greeted me. It was the reporter from the *LA Examiner*. One of his colleagues had been at the site and tipped him off. I gave an honest interview. He liked where I credited my bow work to the practice for my upcoming movie.

"You're getting to be a professional, working in a plug for your new film."

As soon as we hung up, it was the tabloid. His questions led to the splash of blood on the ground from my random hit. Of course, he couldn't allow it to be an accidental hit.

"Bank Robbers Run into Nemesis" would be his headline. This let him bring up the Craig bank robbery. As they say in his industry, if it bleeds, it leads.

I wish Miss Wallace were on the job. She could've handled a lot of this for me.

I called my parents even though it was getting late in Ohio. I had to warn them of the news coming their way.

My mum said, "Rick, for the first time, I'm beginning to understand how my parents must have felt."

That pretty much summed up the conversation.

I didn't feel like watching TV or sleeping, so I rode around. As I drove around the area with my top-down, I listened to "La Bamba", "Rebel Rouser", and "Sweet Little Sixteen", to name a few. It didn't take long for my nerves to settle down. Once I started to feel a little sleepy, I returned to the apartment. Tomorrow would probably be one heck of a day.

Chapter 24

When I woke on Wednesday morning, I didn't immediately get out of bed as was my usual practice. This would be an interesting day, and I had to be very aware of what was happening around me. Today was Wednesday, April 1, 1959. April Fool's Day!

I thought back to last year. Denny had pulled the best one, and it was on Mum of all people. Mum loved reading the newspaper. It was always rolled up and thrown on our front porch. Denny had very patiently taken the newspaper from April 1, 1957, and hid it at the bottom of his least used drawer. Then, on April 1, 1958, he replaced Mum's newspaper with the year-old one.

He was helpful that day, bringing the paper in. Mum was sitting with a cup of tea when we heard, "I thought he died!" She was reading a story about a world leader who had passed in the last year, except the story had him alive. There were continued mutterings.

Finally, there was, "That store is out of business. Why are they advertising?"

Denny's timing was perfect, "Mum?"

"Yes, Denny?"

"April Fool," he practically shouted.

Mum hadn't realized it, but the whole family knew what was happening. Mary probably didn't understand at four, but she knew it was a big secret, and she couldn't giggle until Mum yelled. And did Mum yell? She called Denny every name that could be used in polite company, then chased him down and tickled him. She told him that it was the best joke ever!

The best I ever did was hand Denny a piece of toast at breakfast with what he thought was jelly. I had used red Jello.

This was a day to be wary of all. With the resources of a movie studio, the results could be epic.

I finally surrendered and got out of bed. Then, I had to rush to get back on schedule. I managed to meet Dick for our run at the usual time. Bill at the gate handed me a pink telephone slip. I thanked him and laid it on the seat next to me. I would return the call from the office before reporting to the set.

After parking the car, I glanced at the slip. In large letters, it said, "April Fool!"

It had started.

As I went to the main entrance, I had to walk past the gate, so I gave Bill a wave and said, "Good one."

That's when I noticed he was giving one to almost every incoming car. He gave me a quick smile and returned to his self-appointed duty.

What would John Wayne and company do to me if Bill at the gate could get me so easy?

I was no sooner at the set, and a runner told me I had been summoned to Mr. Monroe's office. I could see the joke starting already, but I had to go. When I got there, it was no joke.

"Rick, you are a natural publicity machine. Your archery session last night has made the national news. The photographers present had pictures of you shooting your bow. I must say that thing looks like a bear to bend. Anyway, we are going to take advantage of this.

"The pictures and story are going to be added to the TV special, which is now one hour. We are going to interview you about how you were trained in archery for your next movie, *Bandits of Sherwood.*"

"When is the special going to be aired?"

"If we can line up sponsors, ABC will air it on Sunday, April 26."

I thought frantically for a minute. That would give us enough time to send new catalogs to our distributors.

"Sir, we have a sponsor, actually two of them."

"How, I mean, who?" he asked.

"Detroit Faucet already has direct product placement in *Sir Nicklaus*, and I know they want to use the show to kick off a national campaign."

"Is this the company you have an interest in?"

"Yes, sir. That's why I know they will sponsor. I will be paying for the sponsorship."

"Okay, who is the other?"

"I need to make a phone call and see if the other party will be ready."

"Anna is on sound stage C right now. You think I don't know what is going on around here?"

"That's why you make what you do, I guess."

"Some days, I wonder if it is enough. Please call Nina and let her know you didn't shoot yourself with an arrow or whatever sort of self-inflicted injuries can happen with a bow."

Since my day was interrupted thoroughly by the president of the studio, I decided to take advantage of it. I caught a ride in one of the messenger's golf carts to sound stage C. The guard reluctantly let me in. The red light was off. If it had been on, I would have never gotten in.

Anna was on a short break. I explained what was going on. She told me she had been in contact with Sally Enright and Mark Downing. They had drawings in the mail for her review. She was ready to be a sponsor for the special. She would announce that she was starting a new product line that evening to drum up some excitement. The actual product would be available in thirty days.

She was planning on doing the rounds of all the TV talk shows to present her new product line. Essentially, she would be selling upscale versions of normal home products. She would only put her name on merchandise that was above average in quality.

I finally made it to the set. I was put in front of the camera almost immediately. It was a series of scenes with Lee Sawyer from the Easterly Ranch. While he wouldn't have a speaking role, it was needed to establish him as a ranch hand to explain his appearance in the stampede.

That took the rest of the morning and all afternoon. Some of the scenes required many takes because of the cast on his arm. It was large, so the camera angles were critical. Lee didn't realize how much he swung his arms around until they kept popping up in the cameraman's viewfinder. Another problem easily solved was his name, Lee.

The ranch foreman was also named Lee in the movie, and the director and writers agreed they didn't want two Lees. That may have been the only time in the entire filming that the director and writers agreed. They ended up calling the real Lee Bobby after his first name, Robert. I joked that his parents should have given him four names to make it Robert Edward Lee Sawyer.

His reply was, "They did."

What do you say to that?

Later, I went to the stunt area for my usual workout. Today wasn't a sword day, so after lifting, I practiced archery. Of course, there were a lot of comments about yesterday.

They ranged from "good shooting" "to even a blind hog."

I held with the "blind hog" myself.

Boxing was fun. My sparring partner was a guy with my reach, speed, and footwork. I couldn't finesse him on anything, so I finally went toe to toe with him. It took four rounds for Coach to call the fight.

"Lessons learned," he called. "Sometimes, you have to wade in and duke it out."

Next was the unarmed combat training. It was getting near the end of my training for the first two belts. I didn't feel like I was some kind of super fighter now, but at the same time, I knew how to react if someone grabbed me.

It wouldn't be pretty, that was for sure. As Coach Palmer explained, this was a practice or lose-it deal. It wouldn't do me any good if I couldn't react from pure reflex. So, I had to figure out how I was going to keep my skills fresh.

Now that I was staying with the studio for another movie, I could advance in my skill levels. I could make the green and probably the brown belt levels while shooting *Bandits of Sherwood*. That wasn't an answer for the long term, but it would do for now.

I stopped by the apartment for a quick shower and then called Nina.

We agreed to have dinner at the Hamburger Hamlet, and I would tell her about my being the reincarnation of Robin Hood. When we arrived, quite a few of her friends were there, so it ended up as story time, with me being the storyteller.

I tried to tell the story straight. When you got down to it, I was stopped in traffic, saw a problem, offered my services, shot five arrows in a minute, and it was done. While trying to give this simple explanation, I kept getting interrupted by kids saying, "But I heard," and then they would go into some fanciful expansion of the story.

The one I liked best was where I said, "I will give them the square of death. When they see how hopeless their position is, they will surrender."

I think it took longer to say that than to shoot. When I was finally able to get the facts out, one kid said it best, "Oh, it wasn't that big of a deal then."

"No, it wasn't," I replied.

I even pointed out that I knew at least three other people in town who could shoot that bow. The only big thing about it was that I happened to be on the scene when my particular skill was needed.

This led to a general discussion of what skills an actor needed to learn. From the conversation, it appeared I had a long way to go. Everything from ballroom dancing to saber dancing was considered necessary for a well-rounded actor. When they found out I wasn't a skilled race car driver or motorcycle rider, it was as though I had let the side down.

I would have to learn as many skills as my interests and time allowed. At the moment, I didn't have time to start anything new.

Nina and I parked in her favorite spot for a while but only necked a little. We talked again about her going to France and then to school in Switzerland. She and her parents had planned this for a long time, so there was no changing it.

We both agreed we were too young to make any life commitments, but we both wanted to part on good terms because one never knew what the future would bring.

We agreed that we would write to each other while we were separated, but I remembered how it went to write to Judy, then Cheryl. As time went by, we would have less in common, so the letters would become fewer and further between until they stopped. It seemed the right way to go when I thought of the drama in breakups at Bellefontaine High School.

Later that night, I read about a guy who accidentally became long-lived. The story starts with him being an old man with some form of dementia, and he starts getting younger with his memories returning. There is a woman who has the same path. The story revolves around them regaining their lives and preparing for the United States' fall. They didn't know why or when it would fall, but forms of government seldom last for more than three hundred years, so they needed to prepare.

They don't know if it will be a gradual change or a sudden event. It was interesting what they had to consider and the foes to overcome. As they become more prepared, others join them as their strengths are recognized. I was looking forward to future stories in the series where they would go off-planet.

Chapter 25

Thursday felt like the next to the last day of school. Everyone on the set was ready to finish up. There was no filming. It was an accounting day. We had to turn in and account for every item that the studio had provided. I didn't have that much. Ellen had accumulated a lot of small items from the wardrobe department. It was easier to leave her hair up and a hat on rather than turning it in at the end of the day.

She asked why she had to return everything.

The studio rep said, "Because I said so."

Everyone present laughed except Ellen. She felt like she was being made fun of. She was. It was that sort of day.

It was all done but the shouting around lunchtime. The cast party will be tomorrow. It wasn't going to be a big event. Sometimes these parties were ballroom affairs. It had been discussed on and off, and the consensus was to have a catered event on the set.

I spent the afternoon, as usual, working out. Today was a sword day. After that, a different set of lifts. I was finished with my boxing lessons. Unarmed combat went quickly. Coach picked up the pace in training. He told me that I was doing very well and learning quickly. I think he just liked finding new ways to throw me around.

Nina had plans with some girlfriends for the evening, so I took a ride out towards Ontario. I turned around at Cucamonga. It was neat seeing the place that Jack Benny talked about in his monologues. When I got home, there was one reporter camped at my door. He was from a tabloid, and I didn't know him. I felt bad because he had been waiting all this time, so I gave a brief interview. We sat out by the pool; it was a pleasant evening.

As usual, he was hunting for a sensational story centered on the latest bank robbers and my bow. I asked him to let me relate the events that happened; then he could form his questions. When I was done, he chuckled for a moment.

"You are so prosaic with how you describe events. Where are the pounding pulse and quickened breath?"

"Uh, there wasn't any. I knew how to shoot the bow; I shot the bow. End of story."

He thanked me and left. It would be the last time I ever felt sorry for a reporter and gave an off-the-cuff interview. His story started with "Cold-Blooded Killer". He wasn't talking about the bank robbers.

My bedtime reading was about a young Texas boy whose father leaves him in charge while he goes on a cattle drive. The boy wants a horse, but Dad tells him he needs a good dog. The next day a dog shows up, but they don't get off to a good start. Later, the dog saves his brother from an angry mama bear.

This starts the bonding process. The dog saves several people over time. In the end, he fights off a mad wolf but, in doing so, contracts rabies. He has to be put down by the boy. This is heart-rending. The boy gets a pup that is the offspring of his friend the dog. Life goes on. I had seen the TV special, but the book was better.

Friday morning started as normal. Exercise and a run. While running, I thought about the loose ends in my life. I had to start house hunting. There was a business office to open here and a contract to sign with Susan Wallace. There was the issue of insurance. How was I even going to get the quotes? That led me to needing a law firm to handle my business.

When I opened an office out here, how would bookkeeping be handled? I couldn't ship everything to Ohio. I needed a business manager to handle these details. At the same time, I didn't want to hire a person and turn my whole life over to them until they earned my trust.

Even then, there had to be checks and balances in place. The studio made this explicitly clear when I signed up for *Sir Nicklaus*. Even though I had done some bit parts previously, it was my first formal work in California.

I had to obtain an entertainment work permit from the state as a child actor. Some of my funds were in a blocked trust, which my parents couldn't touch. That is where my stock market investments resided.

The one thing that had been made clear was that as a minor, I was open to any unscrupulous adults with authority over my life. I was told about Jackie Coogan and how his parents left him broke. I wasn't about to hire some stranger and give him total control over my businesses.

I trusted my parents completely. If they had wanted to steal my money, they'd had plenty of opportunities. It just wasn't going to happen. I wondered if I could get my dad to be my business manager. He didn't know much about running a company, but I trusted him. He could hire help that knew what to do.

There was his housing business in Ohio to consider. How could he run that and take care of my affairs? The answer was clear he couldn't.

Then there was the subject of emancipation. It would benefit the insurance company. Would it benefit Rick Jackson and his family? It was beginning to look like it might benefit me if I could sign my contracts, but what would it do with my relationship with my parents? I would walk away from Hollywood before I would damage my family.

Playing golf with the President of the United States was on my to-do list, followed by starting a new movie. Then there was appearing at the Ohio BSA camporee, and after that, my summer vacation, which I hadn't thought through. I was beginning to wonder if I was losing control of my life.

I didn't have any answers to these questions, but at least I knew I had questions. That was a start. I think a long discussion with my parents was in order. Luckily, I will be in Ohio tomorrow night.

My parents were bringing my golf clubs from Bellefontaine to the hotel. They would be staying overnight. We would be having breakfast with the president at the Ohio State Clubhouse. The kids were being left with Mrs. Hernandez, so we would have time at dinner to have a serious conversation on these issues.

I must say my run went quickly. Dick Wyman, who had been beside me the whole way, wanted to know what had me in an uproar.

"Some personal thoughts," I told him.

"Well, they must have been pretty serious. You just set a personal best for five miles."

"Oh, they were all business-related. I am in a pickle, having business in Ohio and always being here."

"Move everything out here."

"Not so simple. My family isn't that portable."

"How do you know; have you asked them?"

"I have dinner with them tomorrow night. We will discuss it then."

"Then quit borrowing trouble."

That was easier said than done.

When I got to the front gate, Bill had a telephone slip for me, a real one this time. It was to call my agent, Mr. Baxter. I stopped at the office and contacted him. By this time, the people in the office knew me quite well as I had made many a stop. Several times I dropped donuts off as a present for their help.

Mr. Baxter wanted me to know that the Sinatra people had contacted him. They were going to release "Brothers" as the A-side quickly to capitalize on my recent fame for the archery event.

I thought of it as the archery incident. What the heck was I going to call it, "the time I scared the bank robbers out of hiding with my bow and arrow"?

He also told them about the TV special coming out, so they were eager to get the timing right. I stopped by my studio contact's office, Don Pearson. He was sitting with his morning coffee, so I felt free to interrupt. I asked him if he knew anything about my being interviewed about the archery incident.

For once, he was helpful. He told me that it would take less than an hour, and if I could work it in today, he would set it up. We agreed to do it after the party. It wouldn't run late after lunch so we would fit it in.

The party was bittersweet, which I imagine most of those events were. We had come together as a team and worked our way through some problems to make a movie. Now we were all moving on. Some had work lined up. Others didn't. That was the way of this industry. Phone numbers, business cards, and hugs were exchanged, and some gag gifts were presented. No, I'm not sharing why I was given a toilet plunger.

I did make a point of circulating among the entire cast and crew and letting everyone know that I appreciated their help during the production, and I hoped that I would get to work with them again someday. I noticed that some cast members didn't talk with the crew and vice versa. That didn't seem like a good career move for either side.

My role model, John Wayne, had small gifts for everyone. I would do that in the future. He gave mostly bottles of booze. Non-drinkers received a gift certificate from a local grocery. I received a new hat. Mine had been dunked in a trough one too many times. This one was a grey Resistol. He knew my preference for hat makers.

I was too much of a gentleman to mention that it was the studio hat that was ruined. My hats were at home. Now I had white, grey, and black, one for each mood. It is good to be fifteen.

We shook hands, and he told me that he would have a project next year that I might be suitable for. I told him I would be delighted as I planned to hang around town for a while. Now that was interesting. It seems like my unconscious was making some decisions.

I got hugs from Ellen and her mother. They both thanked me for my conduct on and off the set. I had been an unknown to them, and that caused concern. They both assured me Ellen would love to work with me again. That made me think of how Mr. Wayne and Miss O'Hara were a popular movie couple. It was a thought.

After the catered lunch, most of the group departed for local bars to continue the party. I looked up Mr. Pearson, and he took me to the small studio where they had set up to record my interview.

It was pretty straightforward. I told it like it was. The interviewer asked a few questions. I didn't think I would be portrayed as a cold-blooded killer from the tone. I was also learning not to assume what the editors would do.

Later, I caught up with Nina. We went roller skating. It was a fun evening with a bunch of teenagers who acted like teenagers. I was beginning to wonder if I had ever been that young. Well, I was young tonight. We danced on skates and played Crack the Whip until we got whistled off the rink. When they turned the lights down low for a moonlight skate, we snuck a kiss while going around.

Afterward, we stopped at the Hamburger Hamlet for a late-night snack. Skating works up an appetite. I had to get up early for my limo to the airport, so we called it an evening at eleven. I didn't start any new stories.

Chapter 26

Friday morning, I had to skip my run for my early ride to the airport. I almost missed my flight because of the traffic. I don't think they can fit any more cars into Los Angeles; because of this, there wasn't the usual boarding picture at TWA. I walked onto the plane and sat in my first-class seat by the window.

I had to ask a young man in the aisle seat to move so I could get to my seat. He seemed not to care about anyone else in the world. After takeoff, he introduced himself as Paul. He told me how he was meeting his father in Columbus. They were going to be in the gallery and watch President Eisenhower play golf! I told him that sounded like a neat thing to do.

That was a mistake. He kept on and on about how important his family was. I didn't want to be rude, but I finally opened a book and said, "Do you mind?"

There wasn't much he could say to that.

My nose was in that book all the way to Columbus, except when I took a nap.

My parents met me at the gate. After hugs, we went to our hotel. Since this was a short trip, I used a garment bag. They drove up in the Buick. My T-Bird wouldn't have fit us and the golf clubs comfortably. On the way to the hotel, Dad told me that we had to have a serious talk over dinner. I asked what it would be about, but he said it would all wait.

They gave me greetings from my brothers and sister. All was well with them and their schoolwork. Denny was still working on houses that Dad had purchased for the business. He had over two hundred dollars in savings and had plenty of spending money. Eddie was making noises that he would like to have a job where he could earn money.

Mary was still four years old. She couldn't wait to be five in June and all grown up. Her ambition was to get a job at Dog-N-Suds and serve meals on roller skates. I asked Mum about Mary wanting to be a princess.

"Oh, she will wear a tiara while serving meals."

We all agreed that she might grow out of this.

I had been home recently, so there wasn't any other family news. Mr. Stevens from Stevens Construction, who had been on the school board, had been arrested for bribery and corruption in connection with a project to clean the exterior of the courthouse.

After a quick shower to refresh myself and change clothes, I joined my parents in the restaurant.

Dad started with, "Rick, to make sense of what we are thinking about, I have to tell you about a case I was involved in after the war."

Dad was in the Military Police as an investigator. Like every loose body, he had been shipped to the front during the Battle of the Bulge but spent most of his army career as a captain in an investigation unit.

I knew he was an MP, but I had always thought of him in a helmet with a white armband with MP written on it. There were no pictures of him in uniform around the house.

"You were a detective?"

"The army said I was. I never enjoyed it and certainly didn't want to be one after the war. There is another reason that I didn't want to be one. It has to do with my last case."

"What was the case?" I inquired.

"I had to reinvestigate General Patton's death. There were so many questions surrounding it that the army wanted another look. I was brought over from England for an independent look."

"Dad, why did they choose you?"

"I can't prove it, but I think it was because, in my file, there would be notations that I had connections with some very high-level people."

"Who were those?" I naively asked.

"Your godparents," he replied.

I sputtered, "But you never have had any contact. It was more of an accident."

"It doesn't matter. There would have been notes in my file."

"I can remember hearing that there were questions about his death, but I have never heard any details."

"On December 9, 1945, Patton was in a car wreck. His Cadillac was following a lead vehicle. The lead passed a two-and-a-half-ton truck sitting at the side of the road. As the Jeep passed, the truck started up and turned back onto the road right in front of Patton. The general received a broken neck and some head wounds. He was taken to a hospital twenty miles away even though there was one close by.

"Ten days later, he was recovering and was going to be shipped back to the United States. His bags were packed and ready to go. He stood up and dropped dead. It was declared an embolism.

"Now, here are the questionable parts. The truck was driven by a sergeant who was involved in the black market. He was caught later but had taken off after the wreck. The driver of the lead Jeep also disappeared immediately after the incident. He was questioned later but had nothing to say.

"Even though it was early Sunday morning, a general in the local command and his entire staff showed up at the site within minutes. They filed a report. That report disappeared and has yet to surface.

"It is well known that Patton was a rabid anti-communist. The United Nations was just being formed. It was thought that if it became public that the Soviet NKVD caused the incident, the UN would never get off the ground.

"I was brought in to put these rumors to rest. The problem is that I couldn't. Everything could have been coincidental. There was no hard proof either way. Well, that is not quite true. I found a hospital sign-in log with names that I was going to follow up on. The office that I was using in the hospital was broken into, and the log disappeared.

"When I reported this, the investigation was shut down, and I was ordered back to England. Shortly thereafter, I decided I'd had enough. Your mum and I decided to move to the US. We both came from working-class families and had no desire to run with the rich and famous. The fact was that we had little money.

"Your mum went on half-pay with MI6 and has been on call for years but has never had to do anything. I tried railroading, and that wasn't going anywhere. Now you have become wealthy in your own right and allowed us to get a start on making serious money. We have learned a lot about life in the last ten years and want a better one for your brothers and sister.

"There is also the fact that I was involved in that investigation. If those names on that log would have led somewhere, then I'm one of the few people who know anything material about how Patton died. The irony was that I had only glanced at the names before leaving for the day. I was going to start following up the next day. I couldn't even remember them the next morning when I found the log was missing.

"That influenced us to keep a low profile. With your fame, that train has left the station. Now, don't worry about that; it is not your fault you have become famous, and second, there is probably nothing to the whole Patton conspiracy anyway."

I noticed that he had not used the word accident once.

"So, Mum and Dad, what is this leading up to?"

"We are going to move to California."

I can't describe what went through me. My body seemed to shudder, and I let out a huge sob. I gasped for breath a couple of times. It felt like a weight had been lifted, and I was free.

"Rick, are you okay?" Mum and Dad asked at the same time.

"I am, but it feels like something wonderful has happened like I had a big spring coiled up in me, and it just came unwound in a good way. I'm all for it for a bunch of reasons. Why are you?"

"We think we can be more secure there."

"Why do you think we will be more secure there?"

"Rick, have you looked at any of the houses in Beverly Hills, especially those upon the mountains?"

"Oh, I see what you mean. Some of them are virtual fortresses, and it would look really weird to have something like that in Bellefontaine."

"We are thinking of a fenced compound with a gatehouse, guest house, swimming pool, and all the amenities."

"Can I live with you?"

"That's another reason we want to move to California. We all miss you," said Mum. Then she added, "Rick, why don't you go wash your face? You have tears running down your cheeks."

I left the table for the men's room. The only reason for my state that I could think of was that I had been lonely and stressed out.

I didn't even know it until relief was in sight. I would have to think this through later. What if they hadn't said they were moving to California? Would I have just kept getting wound tighter and tighter until I snapped?

When I returned to the table, we continued talking about why they should move to California.

Dad continued, "There is also a practical reason. You are planning on buying a house. I have talked to the accountants. It would make more sense to have everything in a company name. Even your cars would help with insurance rates. We could pay rent to live there if you bought the house we can't afford."

"Stop right there, Dad. You will not be paying rent."

"We don't want to be freeloaders."

"You won't, Dad. You will be earning it as my business manager. I assume you are going to sell the housing business. If you leave the area, you will need something to do. I need a trustworthy business manager, so it works out well."

"I can do that; we wondered what I would do after the move. As far as selling the company, we are keeping it. I have talked to several local realtors about handling the rental portion. The office can continue to handle maintenance. Grimes will audit the books."

Dad continued, "The company isn't worth as much as you might think. It gives us a fantastic cash flow, but we also owe a lot for those houses. As equity has built up, I have used it to purchase new units. I think it is time to quit buying and start paying off those houses.

"If they were all paid for, the company would be worth half a million dollars; however, there is three hundred thousand in debt. As each mortgage is retired, the money can go towards paying off the others. I estimate that they will all be paid for in five years. After that, your mother and I will have an income of thirty thousand a year over and above our current income."

"This will be great," I gushed.

"When you fly back Monday, Jack will go with you," Mum told me.

"My apartment has two bedrooms, one of which is an office right now. I can buy a bed for Dad while he hunts for a house. If he doesn't mind, he can use my car out there during the day for his business."

"I thought we could do something like that."

"Mum and Dad, the more I think of this, the better it is. I can see with business, my acting, and everything else I have been doing, I haven't had much of a life, at least a kid's life. It has been almost all work and no play. If Nina hadn't dragged me out to eat, I would never have interacted with any kids my age."

Our discussion on the logistics of buying a house, setting up an office, the proper staffing, and moving took up several more hours. It was late when I went to my room. I went to bed and slept immediately.

Sunday morning, we were up, dressed, and in the restaurant to meet the president for breakfast. President Eisenhower came in almost to the minute. We shook hands all around.

You could tell the president didn't remember Mum and Dad that well, but that was to be expected. They spent several minutes sorting out how he had become my godfather. You could see it click when he remembered. Dad and the president also exchanged looks as though they had just remembered something but let it go.

"That's right; you were Elizabeth's bodyguard during the war, saved her life, and became her friend."

Looking at Dad, he said, "Jack, you were a captain at the time, and now it comes back that you were involved in the second investigation of Patton's death. Bad business that. I know at the time, we were concerned that you could become a target if the Soviets were involved. Then, you decided to retire and move back to Ohio. We had Army Intelligence keep tabs on you for a few years, but it was all quiet, so that was discontinued around 1951."

Mum said, "It must have been your people hanging around. In 1950, one of them tried to come into our kitchen at night. He changed his mind at the last moment. He will never know how close he came to death."

Ike responded, "It was shortly after that coverage was discontinued. That agent changed his mind because he heard the slide being pulled back on a weapon. It was decided you didn't need any help."

My parents and the president exchanged tight smiles. They all knew how close to a disaster they had come. Ike (anyone who had ever met him would always remember him as Ike) changed the subject.

"Rick, that hairdryer you sent to Mamie was a big hit. The White House staff wants them for themselves and as visitor gifts. I have been ordered to buy thousands of them with the White House logo. How do I do that?"

"Sir, they will have to be ordered from American Style, as they now hold the license."

Dad broke in. "I have their contact information. Who should I pass it to?"

Ike signaled an aide who was sitting near us to write down the information from Dad.

Dad said, "I will forewarn them. This should make their day."

Ike wanted to know what my long-term plans were. I told him about my interest in space. He thought this was normal for a boy of my age. NASA had been formed last year after the Sputnik launch.

He told me if I were interested, he could arrange for me to meet Werner Von Braun in Huntsville. I told him I would love to do that. Again, the ever-present aide was charged with arrangements.

After that, we went out to play golf. It was a beautiful day. I was a little surprised that Mr. King, Judy's dad, was in the foursome. When I thought about it, it made sense that a local businessman of his stature would be invited. Our fourth was Ohio State Auditor James Rhodes. I was introduced to him, and Mr. King and I explained how we knew each other. Mr. Rhodes took more of an interest in me when he realized my connections.

Mr. King told me he appreciated the hairdryer Dad sent him. It helped make the women in his life more punctual, which was a good thing.

He also told me that Don Thompson and Paul Samson said "Hi" and if I had any more projects, let them know.

Mr. King dryly continued, "I suspect the fact that the bonus you sent them let them both buy a house helped their enthusiasm."

I told him I wasn't working on anything at the moment but would keep them in mind. They had done a really good job for me.

I asked how Judy was doing.

Her dad pointed to the gallery and said, "Why don't you ask her."

There she was, looking more mature and beautiful than ever. She was growing up. I went over, and she rushed to my arms for a big hug. As she hugged me, I felt something dig into my chest. When we parted, I looked down and saw a class ring wrapped in angora on a chain. Well, that answered that. We exchanged greetings, but it was obvious that anything we had was in the past.

As I turned to return to the tee, I saw the guy who I had been sitting next to on the plane. I thought about being a smart ass and winking at him. Instead, I went over and shook his hand, then led him over to the president and introduced him to the group.

It was quick, as we had to tee off, but from the look on his face, I had done the right thing. The guy jumping around and waving had to be his dad. I don't know what their relationship was, but from the look on his dad's face, I know it just got better.

I didn't set any course records, but I beat everyone else. For some reason, I felt relaxed and smooth all day long. I walked most of the day with the president, and he showed an interest in my activities. He commented that I would have been a good officer in the war.

After the round and another promise from the president to be at the camporee if he could, we parted company. We drove back to Bellefontaine for the night with plans to return by limo early in the morning for Dad's and my flight to LAX.

Chapter 27

Dad and I had to leave Bellefontaine at 4 a.m. to make our flight from Dayton. Dad told me it was the first time he had flown first class. I'm not sure that he got the full experience, as we both slept most of the way to Los Angeles. I had the studio arrange a limo for us before I left on the trip, so it was a smooth ride.

It was around five o'clock California time when we got to my apartment. After dropping our bags off, we drove to S. S. Kresge. There we bought a single bed, mattress, and bedding for Dad to use. We had to put the T-Bird top-down and have the bed stick almost straight up in the back seat. Dad commented that we looked like hillbillies driving around Beverly Hills.

Returning to the apartment, the phone was ringing. It was Nina wanting to know how my trip to Ohio and playing golf with the president went. I gave her a brief description of the events. When she found out that my dad was with me, she insisted that we attend a small dinner party they were having on Thursday evening.

Upon my telling her that Dad was here to house hunt, she got all excited. What is it with women and house hunting? She wanted to know if we had a realtor yet, and when I replied that we didn't, she recommended that I get to my studio liaison first thing in the morning as the studio had a couple on retainer.

As Dad set up and made his bed, I made a quick trip to In-N-Out. When I returned with burgers and fries, Dad was on the phone with Mum, letting her know we had arrived okay. After that, we called it a day. It had been a long one. It was now ten o'clock, and we had been up since 1 a.m. California time. There was no reading tonight!

I left for my run on Tuesday morning while Dad was drinking his coffee. As usual, I met Dick Wyman on the high school running track. After our run, he stopped by the house, and I introduced him to Dad. They seemed to receive each other well. Dad thanked Dick for keeping an eye on me. Dick told him I had been no problem, and he would tell Dad all the good stuff later.

Of course, I had to say "Hey!" to that.

They both laughed. Boy, I was easy.

Dad explained to Dick that he was on a preliminary house-hunting mission. He was to select several candidates, and then Mum would fly out, and they could make the final decision together. I noticed that I wasn't included in that decision, and that was simply fine with me. It was nice to be a kid again.

It wasn't that I wanted to regress to being a small kid again. It was just nice not to have all the adult pressures on me. I suppose, like all teenagers, I wanted to be treated as an adult. That was fine. It was all the responsibility that went with it that was no fun.

I started the day with a bagel for breakfast with cream cheese, orange juice, and coffee. In Bellefontaine, I had never heard of a bagel. I read about them but had never seen them for sale, much less eaten them. Dad would make us a full breakfast of bacon, eggs, hash browns, juice, coffee, and toast. I could get used to this having a parent around.

After cleaning up, we went to the studio. Dad agreed that we should use their realtor if we could. I checked Dad in at the studio front office, getting him a temporary pass. That was a little weird, having to sign for my dad.

From there, we went to Mr. Pearson's office. His attitude had changed since the last time I had seen him. I think maybe Mr. Monroe had a few words with him. It didn't matter. He was helpful this morning. He was very respectful to my father and listened to me when I told him what we needed.

He asked a few questions about what sort of house we were looking for. Dad described it. To his credit, Mr. Pearson never blinked. He must be used to this sort of thing.

"You will want to deal with Long & Coster. They handle the high-end properties in Beverly Hills."

He made a phone call and set an appointment for Dad after lunch.

Since we had several hours to kill and *Sir Nicklaus* was wrapped up, I had the time to give him a studio tour. I was to start my week of intense unarmed combat training for my grey belt right after lunch. This worked out well, considering I hadn't planned anything.

During the tour, I was amazed at the number of people I had met while filming. These were mostly crew members. They were using the fake boxcar top to re-shoot an earlier scene. I was recognized by the key grip, who praised me after being introduced to Dad.

"Ricky saved this scene for us."

Dad smiled and looked at me, "I knew you wouldn't give up inventing things. What is your next moneymaker?"

I hadn't given it any thought since I had been so busy with the film. I would have to keep my eyes open for opportunities.

I took Dad over to the costume and makeup department. Sometimes things just work out. They were finishing up several ladies in Civil War-era dresses. They had used the hairdryer on the men next to them but had these enormous rollers in the lady's hair. They called them tin can rollers because, originally, women used empty cans for the task.

"Hey, Rick, why don't you make us something to hurry up this process?" said Melba, one of the makeup artists.

Dad started to sputter as he laughed.

"Well, now I know what the next invention will do," he said between chuckles.

We ran into Mr. Monroe doing a walk around, so I took the opportunity and introduced him to my father. Mr. Monroe expressed his pleasure at meeting Dad and told him he would tell him the stories about me later.

I responded with "Hey!" Both he and Dad laughed. Boy, I'm easy.

"Seriously, Jack. Nina told me she invited you to our dinner party on Thursday. We can talk more then, and I can tell you about your fine young son then."

Dad expressed his eagerness to Sam for the party, and we moved on.

As soon as Mr. Monroe was out of sight, he asked me, "What do we wear to these things? Do I have to rent a tux?"

"No, Dad, you are dressed fine right now. Sport coat and short sleeves or golf shirts are good out here."

"Good, your Mum told me it would be, but this place is something else."

I next gave him a tour of the stunt area. Again, I was surprised by the number of people I had met on the lot. Once more, there were kind words expressed about my work ethic. Dad beamed a lot. It made me glad that I had pushed myself to achieve as much as possible.

Coach Palmer wasn't in yet, so I couldn't introduce Dad to the guy who liked throwing me around. We had lunch in the commissary. It had the usual extras in costumes. Today must have had a World War II movie going on because there were a lot of G.I.s. Dad told me this brought some old times back. Not all bad, not all good, just old times.

I couldn't resist it when I handed Dad my car keys. "Return it with a full gas tank and drive carefully, and if you get pulled over for speeding, don't call me to bail you out."

I heard Dad muttering as he left, "Maybe Peg did the wrong one."

Coach Palmer was ready for me when I got to his area. After changing and performing my limbering-up exercises, he showed me I had a lot to learn. We went at it for the rest of the day, not quitting until six o'clock. Fortunately, I had told Dad that it was scheduled to run this late, so he didn't have to wait long.

He was excited. He had toured two properties, and both would do, but the second one was perfect, at least to him. Mum might have a different opinion. He was scheduled to look at two more tomorrow. There were not that many houses, or as Dad was calling them, estates, on the market at any given time.

We had dinner at the Brown Derby. I introduced Dad to Mr. Cobb. Yet again, Dad was told what a fine son he had. Dad beamed some more but did ask me how many people I had to pay off for all the good comments. Mr. Cobb even had a picture of me and Mr. Sinatra on the wall. It had been taken when he joined me at my table. I hadn't even noticed the flashbulb going off.

Over dinner, Dad told me that he had contacted the American Style people and told them of the request from the White House. Ike's aide had already contacted them, so they were aware. To say they were excited was to put it mildly. They had never had a product launch like this before. They were having the hairdryer housings made on the prototype molds, so they would be at the White House as soon as the first production went to market.

After dinner, Dad drove me around to show off the two "estates". We couldn't see them as they had walls around them and a manned gate at the entrance. Both houses were empty, but the guard service was still in place. I wondered if I would ever get my car keys back.

Dad called Mum after we got home. He told her what he had seen so far. She decided to fly out on Friday to review what Dad had picked. Mrs. Hernandez was available to watch over the kids. From what I could pick up, she was outstaying her welcome at the Wingers. It didn't look like her husband would soon leave Castro's jail. You would have thought that since Batista had jailed him, Castro would have let him out, but since he was working for a free elected government, neither dictator wanted him free.

Mrs. Winger was tired of having her brother-in-law's wife staying with them. Because of this, Mrs. Hernandez jumped at every chance she could get to stay at our house. While she didn't ever say it, I think Mrs. Hernandez wanted out as much as Mrs. Winger wanted her out.

That night I read more about how the markets worked. I decided to be a long-term investor because short-term buys and sell risks were not to my liking. The idea of selling short gave me the heebie-jeebies. The idea of hoping something would fail would drive me batty.

Chapter 28

When it came to commodities, I could see myself failing to sell a grain option and receiving a call from the yardmaster that my grain car had arrived. The only way I would do commodities is gold in the safe. Now that is a comforting thought.

Wednesday had the normal start. It was a little rainy out but not cold at all, so Dick and I did our morning run. It was nice coming home to Dad fixing breakfast. I had put the coffee pot on when I first got up. I was going to gain weight if Dad kept fixing his heart attack specials. I enjoyed the meal. Best of all, I wasn't alone. I hadn't realized how much I missed people.

Dad dropped me off at the studio as he was off to see two more houses today. I spent the day with Coach Palmer. I was finally feeling comfortable with what we were doing. Repetition is everything as you develop muscle memory. To be good, it almost had to be a way of life.

I only wanted to be good enough to survive if I needed the skills. I had read somewhere that better was the enemy of good enough. The author's point was that once something was good enough, you should go with it. You could spend the rest of your life making it better but would never get the job done.

One of my Civil War essays in school was on Union General George McClellan. He had built and organized a powerful army but would never use it. He wanted to make it better. You have to wonder how many people died because he wouldn't take decisive steps early in the war.

Thinking these deep thoughts also took me out of the events of the moment. I came back to the moment in mid-air just as I was about to slam onto the mat. So much for deep thoughts.

We did a break for lunch in that circus we called the commissary. Today, it was zoot suits and Cavaliers. A couple of tables over, I was being eyed by a couple of Cleopatra's handmaidens. They had wraps over their costumes, but they seemed to come open every time I glanced their way. They were also too old; they must have been twenty-five or even older! It was hard to tell with all the heavy makeup they had to wear.

I decided to enjoy the show but not attempt to sample the wares. I may be a hick kid from Ohio but could tell trouble when I saw it. The room was getting much warmer when they left with one last flash and a laugh. I had to delay leaving until my body settled down.

After lunch, we spent time going through diagrams of different techniques until our meals settled. I couldn't beat Coach, but I was holding my own for longer and longer. I began to realize that I was larger than him and stronger, but his skills made up for the difference. We went at it for the rest of the afternoon.

During the lesson, people stopped by and gave useful suggestions, such as, "Tear his head off, Rick," or "Don, kick his butt."

I very quickly learned to ignore all of this, or the Coach would send me flying or force me to slap the matt in submission. The day ended with all my body parts attached, so I counted it as a victory. Bruises don't count. That was another thing I noticed. Coach Palmer could judge exactly how much force to use so I wasn't damaged, only bruised. Well, maybe my pride. I had to go all out; if I ever connected, I could hurt him.

I asked him if he was concerned about me hurting him.

His reply was, "Good luck with that."

I had a long way to go.

While waiting for Dad to pick me up, I gave some thought to those hair rollers that the makeup artists were using on the women's hair. It didn't seem like a big deal to me to modify an existing curling iron to heat with electricity. It would be a lot faster than letting hair dry around a roller.

It would solve one of my pet peeves. I hated the sight of women with their hair in rollers covered by a plastic scarf out in public. It just looked unsightly. A man wouldn't go out without shaving or combing his hair. Why should women run around looking like that?

While the bee-hive hairdos didn't turn me on, I must say I did like that upswept look where the hair turned up at the sides. It was like those hats nuns wore that looked like they had wings on their heads. It made them look like they were about to fly away. Now that was a thought, flying nuns. Nah.

I couldn't modify an existing curling iron, for there was no room for a heating element. I would start with an aluminum tube and go from there. I wondered if the prop shop would let me work there.

Dad was excited. He thought he had found the perfect property. It sat on ten acres of land. It was a seventeen-bedroom mansion. What would we do with seventeen bedrooms? Once Dad explained the deal, it sounded like a winner from the price point of view. Normally, the house would sell for almost two million dollars. However, the bank wanted to get rid of it, and it needed a lot of work.

The bank had six hundred thousand in it and would be glad to get their money out of it and move on. Dad figured it would take almost another two hundred thousand dollars to bring it back to a first-rate condition, but it would be worth a bundle when it was done.

Because of the value of the property, the bank kept the guard service on. The realtor had arranged with the security company to let him and me back in so I could see inside. Dad told me more about the house as he drove us in my car. It had two master-bedroom suites, one at each end of the floor, and six other suites, three to a side, all on the second floor. A third floor had the other nine bedrooms and four baths.

The ground floor had a dining room, a library, and a kitchen with an enormous pantry. There was a large room that could be used as a ballroom or for parties, a formal sitting room, a breakfast room, and several side parlors.

There were front and back stairs. It was what I thought of as a mansion. An extra-tall, double-wide front door opened into a large foyer. In the center of the foyer was a grand marble staircase to the second floor.

The staircase would be perfect for Mary to make a grand entrance at her coming-out ball. These were Dad's words, not mine. I think he was excited about the possibilities. I wondered how Mum would feel about all this.

Dad continued telling me about the house. There was a large swimming pool with a bathhouse. The garages were on the side and would hold seven vehicles. There was a loft over the garage for the chauffeur. Now I know Dad was losing it.

An eight-foot wall surrounded the property. The house sat on the inside of a hairpin road. The gated entrance was at the top of the climbing hairpin. The lower side of the property went right to the lowest edge of the hairpin. The walls didn't. There was enough room between the walls and the road at that point that a small three-bedroom ranch house had been built between the walls and the road.

This house was part of the entire parcel for sale.

Before Dad could ramble on much more, we arrived. The guard was the same one who had been on duty earlier, so he waved us in. When Dad told me there was a guardhouse, I had pictured a small building at the gate. That building was there, but it was a small wing of a unit designed for live-in guards, or more like the arrangements at a firehouse.

Dad hadn't described the exterior. The best I could come up with was English Tudor brick. When I asked Dad about it, he told me it was supposed to remind one of Somerset House in England, but not so grand. Another house with fifty-three rooms in California had the same style, the Kohl house up near San Francisco.

This one only had seventeen rooms. It was a beautiful red brick with white blocks accenting each corner. At one end of the building was a six-story tower that must have a wonderful view of downtown LA.

Chapter 29

I asked Dad about the history of the house. He told me how it had been built in 1925 for Jason Talmadge, an heir to a railroad fortune of a hundred million dollars. Talmadge was considered a wastrel with an extremely bad reputation and had disappeared from his yacht one night near Catalina Island. He was known as a strong swimmer, but they were shark-infested waters.

His body was never recovered. It took seven years to have him declared dead. He was the last of his line and had no will, so his estate reverted to the state of California, which auctioned off the property.

It had a checkered history after that, with no owner keeping it for more than seven or eight years. It had enormous upkeep costs. The last owner had quit making payments to the bank, so it was repossessed. I asked Dad how we would be able to afford the upkeep.

"We won't. We will fix this place up and sell it for over a million. Then, we will use the profit to buy and pay cash for a more reasonable house. We couldn't afford the upkeep anyway."

There went my dream of living in a mansion.

The landscaping had been kept under control but could use a lot of work. Dad had taken a quick look around earlier. The most expensive item he had noted was the electric wiring that needed to be updated.

Once inside, while it needed a lot of paint, it was in surprisingly good condition. At least there was no sign of water leakage or mold. Those were what we looked for when buying a rental property. There was no evidence of large or small running or flying critters, which was a plus. The marble flooring in the foyer would need serious polishing, but it would be gorgeous.

There was old furniture sitting around, but it was all in poor condition. Just like in our rental houses, people left stuff rather than having it hauled away. No individual room had much, but when added up, it would take a lot of work to remove it all.

When we toured the kitchen, it was obvious that we needed all new appliances. As we went, we checked out the plumbing in the many bathrooms we found downstairs. Upstairs were the eight-bedroom suites. They each had a bedroom, bathroom, and sitting room. The closets were so large you could walk into them.

Each bathroom had a shower and a tub. The tubs were sunken into the floor and could hold several people. The showers needed adjustable showerheads. The master bedroom had a small dining area, a reading nook with a fireplace, and other amenities. Dad figured Mum would want to live there.

The third floor had the other nine bedrooms and four baths. One loses count after a while. Guys do, anyway. I bet any female I have ever met could draw a complete diagram of the house after one trip. This included Mary.

There was a fourth floor with servant's quarters. They were decent. They were made for live-in servants, so they were more on the bedroom suites order. Last, we went down to the basement. It was huge. There was a furnace room with the largest coal-fired furnace I had ever seen. Dad had it marked down for replacement with a gas furnace. The wine cellar racks were empty.

There would be plenty of room to put in a ping-pong table. We would shoot pool in the billiards room next to the library. The billiard table and a pool table had been left in place. They were probably too heavy to move out. The basement was long enough that we could install a bowling alley if we wanted.

The library was classic. It had built-in bookshelves to the ceiling. There were rolling ladders to reach the higher shelves. Dad and I were standing there admiring it. He was leaning against the ornate fireplace mantel. As we started to leave, Dad pushed away and, in doing so, hit a button hidden in the scrollwork. A set of bookshelves next to the fireplace swung open. We had a secret passage!

Dad stuck his head in the newly opened doorway. He flicked a light switch inside the passage. It lit up the tunnel and revealed a set of stairs going down. He searched around and found a lever which opened the door from the inside. We tested it with me on the outside and Dad on the inside. We didn't want to leave it open for a guard to find, and we didn't want to lock ourselves in.

After closing the door and testing it one more time, we descended. It was a long way beyond the depth of the basement. We came out into a dry room. A set of light switches was at the bottom of the steps. Switched on, they revealed a room every bit as big as the basement.

This room was furnished. All the furniture was covered with sheets to protect them from dust. We looked under a couple of the sheets. The furniture was in excellent condition for stuff made in the 1920s. That is to say, while functional, it was really out of style. Unlike the basement above us, the floor was wood. That seemed weird, the basement being above us.

We explored the sub-basement. All the walls were plastered and painted white. There was a fireplace in a sitting area. The room looked to be as big as the full basement above. In one corner, we found a set of stairs going up.

We went up those stairs, which were even longer than those going down. At the top of these stairs was a long passage with several branches. We went to the end of the first branch. At the end of the branch, there was a door on either side with a small peephole in the center of each door.

Peering through the peepholes, you looked into the sitting room of a bedroom suite. A little more exploring found that all the bedroom suites on the second floor had a concealed doorway that gave access to the hidden sub-basement.

We returned to the sub-basement and checked the rest of it out. There was another set of stairs, but they led down. Turning on more lights, we descended these steps and followed a long tunnel that dead-ended with a door. In the end, a peephole looked out into the dark. Dad took a chance and opened the door.

It opened in the back of a closet that held mops and brooms. When Dad opened that door, we found ourselves in a garage. Looking out the windows in the garage, we realized we were standing in the house outside of the walled area.

Dad turned to me and said," What do you think, Rick? Should we buy it?"

"You're kidding. Of course, we have to buy it. This is so neat."

"Well, it is neat, but I was thinking of the security aspects."

"Oh yeah, Dad, I thought of that right away."

Well, maybe after he mentioned it; nice move, Exlax.

He let me off with a smirk.

We continued exploring the sub-basement. It was divided into several areas by walls. The areas weren't closed off like rooms; they were more like bays. The first bay we looked at contained a bar. It looked like the bar itself was made from mahogany or some other expensive wood. Any bottle that had been opened was empty. The contents long ago evaporated, leaving a nasty-looking residue.

Those that were sealed seem to be fine. Dad shook his head over one bottle of Scotch. It was labeled as being fifty years old. The label showed that it had been bottled in 1874.

Dad said, "This is almost enough to make me start drinking again, but not enough."

He then put the bottle down gently.

The next bay had a bed. There were interesting items on the shelves around the bed. They included whips and chains and other things. I couldn't begin to guess how they might be used. I had read of such things but never thought to see them. Maybe Talmadge was in chains when he took his midnight swim.

The last bay was a small office with a roll-top desk and a safe. The safe had a mammoth door, which looked like it would take dynamite to open. Dad rummaged around the roll-top desk. He prodded and pulled the wooden decorations around the drawers and pigeonholes. He was rewarded for his efforts by opening a small hidden drawer.

Dad told me, "I have never seen an old roll-top desk without these secret compartments."

The drawer only held a slip of paper. The paper had numbers and letters, 54L after passing twice, 62R, and 15L after passing thrice, finishing with 84R, which proved to be the combination to the safe.

The safe contained old money. They were the large bills that used to be issued. There were twenty bundles of one-hundred-dollar bills. Each bundle had fifty bills. We looked at the bills in several of the bundles. It seemed no two were alike.

Some had blue seals, others red. Some serial numbers started with stars, others with numbers. Although they all said, "One Hundred Dollars", they were drawn on many different banks. Some said they would be repaid in gold. Others stated that interest would be paid. They had pictures of people I had never heard of.

Dad and I were silent while examining this treasure trove. There were ten large certificates, which were titled "United States Bearer Bond". They had a face value each of one million dollars.

On top of the bonds lay a bank savings book. It was from a Swiss bank and had an account number but no name. Lightly written in pencil was a long number which was probably the password for the account. There was no notation in the book of how much was on deposit.

Dad and I just looked at each other. This was almost too much to comprehend.

Dad finally said, "Maybe we can afford the upkeep on this place after all. In the meantime, let's lock up and get out of here before the guards realize they can't find us."

After making copies for each of us of the safe combination, Dad replaced the original in its compartment. After checking through the peephole, we turned out the lights and exited the hidden area. I checked my watch. It felt like we had been in there for a lifetime. It had been an hour.

As Dad drove us back to my apartment, we discussed what we had found. Dad's position was that no matter what he thought of Ike as a person now, he didn't want to give him the money!

We had three separate issues: cash, bearer bonds, and a Swiss bank account. We had no idea what the law entailed. Dad and I had both been raised with the philosophy of finders-keepers, so we weren't in a hurry to share with anyone, or as Dad said, "Give it to Ike."

Maybe Mum's title would come in handy. Everyone in America expected the British nobility to be wealthy. In the meantime, I was known to have money. Because of this, if we were discreet, no one would know how much we had or where.

Dad would be making a full asking price offer for the house and its contents as soon as he could tomorrow. He suspected the bank would jump at it. We felt no compunction about not telling the bank what they were selling. It was the bank's job to value the property, not ours.

Our ethical grounds were shaky, and we both knew it. When you got down to it, we had just found out what our price was. I wondered what Mum would think of the whole thing. Upon returning home, I found out after Dad had called her.

She would be on a plane on Friday to inspect our new house on Saturday. We weren't to breathe a word of our find to anyone—as if we were planning to. She would call a friend in England to have them investigate our legal responsibilities.

She would also have them check into how to discreetly cash in the bearer bonds and obtain access to the Swiss bank account. Mum didn't want anyone in the U. S. to have any idea of what we found. Even her friend wouldn't be told how much was involved. I suspected her friend was my godmother.

Dad and I talked late into the night about how this sudden change would affect our lives. Other than the house, there couldn't be many outward changes. That would raise questions. My biggest thought was I could have a nice workshop in the corner of the basement.

I think Dad was stunned. In one year, he had gone from working on the extra board on the railroad, barely keeping food on the table, to being a respectable business owner, and now to a small fortune, and depending on the Swiss account, maybe a large one. He kept coming back to the thought that he would have to run my business because he would have nothing else that needed doing.

There was the fact that the British nobility would be living in a small castle with a movie star son. That would have social implications. How would we handle that? We both found that we would leave that one to Mum; it was her darned title, so it was her problem. Frankly, we were both scared to death of what would be coming our way.

I had a hard time getting to sleep, but when I tried to read, I couldn't. I would read a paragraph and have no idea what I had just read, so I gave up. Sometime during the night, I fell asleep. I had set the alarm and was glad I had done so. I felt like crap.

Chapter 30

My exercises and morning run with Dick helped a lot. At least, I was now fully awake. Coffee made me human once more. Dad dropped me off at the studio so he could stop at the realtor's and start the purchase process.

I spent the entire day in the stunt area. Most of it was with Coach practicing hand-to-hand. During breaks when he had to attend to other business, I lifted weights and then had some swordplay with Sammy. I also shot several hundred arrows. Well, I shot the bow several hundred times after retrieving arrows.

I was even called on to be a sparring partner for an actor training for a part as a boxer. I must say he has to be a better actor than a boxer. He was nice but in his thirties and married, so we had little in common. As far as size, we were evenly matched.

Coach told me they would need some extras in the movie, and I could pick up a film credit if I appeared as a sparring partner in his training camp. I told him to check on it for me. If the timing was right, it might be fun.

Even with these diversions, I spent a lot of time practicing hand-to-hand. Coach told me I was progressing and would be the equivalent of a Marine green belt by the end of the week. By the end of filming *Bandits of Sherwood*, he had hopes of getting me to brown belt level.

I was waiting for Dad when he pulled up in my T-Bird. I wondered if I would ever get to drive my car again.

Dad was chipper. "I made the offer, and they accepted. Since it is a cash deal, this will go quickly. I signed the papers so that they could check on the finances of Jackson Holdings to prove that the company is a good credit risk. They even asked for a copy of the contract for your next film.

"The only thing that puzzled them was that my offer included the contents. They figured we would want the place cleaned out. I blamed it on Mum. I told them she hadn't seen the contents yet, but when she heard there was furniture left behind, she insisted on seeing it first. They couldn't sign off fast enough after that."

"Oh dear, how will we ever be able to afford to have all that cleaned out," I said in my most plummy British accent.

Dad swatted me up the side of the head.

We cleaned up and went to Monroe's dinner party. There were half a dozen guests and their spouses, mostly business types, but Anna Romanov was there. She and Nina were sitting next to each other. Dad and I sat across from them. We were at the far end. Anna had been invited as she knew Dad and made the numbers even.

Anna told us how happy she was with Sally Enright at DF. She had come through with some spectacular designs that would start a lot of conversations about her product lines.

Nina asked Dad how our house hunting was going. When he told her he had made an offer on the Talmadge Estate, she and Anna both were excited. They had always wondered about it but hadn't been in it. Dad told them that Mum was coming out on Friday, and they were welcome to tour the house with us on Saturday.

They both gave an enthusiastic yes. After dinner, Mr. Monroe was brought up to date on events. He offered a studio limo to pick Mum up at the airport and drive us all to the house on Saturday. That took care of the logistics nicely. Dad thanked him. Mr. Monroe took Dad off to show him his cigar collection. Miss Romanov accompanied them, so suddenly Nina and I were alone.

We necked for a while, but it wasn't with desperate passion. We knew she would be leaving soon and didn't want to turn it into a tragedy. Our budding romance was returning to friendship. I wondered if it would eventually descend to an old acquaintance. Of course, there was a song about that. We have sung it every New Year's Eve.

After we returned to the apartment, Dad and I continued our conversation about the move to California and opening a business office here. Between those two items, there were hundreds of details. Dad was also smart enough not to come to any firm conclusions on the move without Mum's input. He figured the basic plan would be to start the house repairs and let the kids finish out the school year in Ohio before moving. Luckily, I had adapted to California, and the others were young enough that the move wouldn't be traumatic.

It was hard for me to think of being in high school anymore. I needed the formal paperwork and certainly the basic knowledge from high school, but the idea of sitting in class all day long was dreadful. If I had my way, I would push through high school as fast as possible with private tutors, whatever it took.

That night I reread an old favorite. When Delmaire is murdered, Baley and Olivaw are sent to Solaria to solve the murder and learn about Solarian society and how it works.

Friday was an even nicer day than most California days. The weather and temperature were perfect. The sky was clear, and you could see snow on the mountaintops. Seeing this and knowing how short the drive was to the beach reminded me of why California was going to grow in the next few years.

Dick and I had a good run. I tried to talk Dad into joining us, but that was a lost cause. At least he had given up smoking and drinking. Dad dropped me off. His plans for the day were to make certain the house deal was on track and then check on the status of the Susan Wallace contract.

She had had it in her hands for several days now. It was about time for her to sign or get clarification on anything she wasn't certain of. He was also going to start looking for offices.

Besides the offices, we needed to retain a law firm, sort out the insurance policy issues, and look for a local bookkeeper. We would also need an accounting firm to audit our books. I would need an engineering group to work on my inventions or hire engineers. Then there was a need for a patent attorney closer than Ohio. The list seemed to go on and on. Thank goodness my Dad would be looking into these for me.

My day was similar to yesterday. I shot a lot of arrows, lifted weights, banged metal with Sammy, then flew through the air with Coach Palmer or pounded on the mat to make him stop hurting me. It was a good day, in other words.

I did find the time to go to the prop shop. Mr. Rodrigues told me that I could work with whatever I wanted. He would have to charge me if I used too many raw materials. When I told him what I was trying, he told me not to worry about the materials. If I wanted to build a whole house, then we would talk. I thanked him and got to work.

The electric curling iron would be a simple tool. It needed a straight portion about ten inches long and a two-inch outside diameter. There would be a clamp to hold the curl tight while heating and forming the hair into a curl.

There would have to be a temperature control so the iron wouldn't overheat and burn the hair. I used an aluminum tube for the straight portion or heating tube as I thought of it. Then, using a band saw, I cut another tube in half to act as the clamp. I was smart enough to make a fixture to hold the tube by its end while cutting it in half.

After cutting eight inches, I stopped and then sawed that portion off the base stock. Now, I had a curved piece to fit against the heating tube. It was far from a good fit but good enough for my rough prototype. How do you fasten the clamp to the heating tube and adjust it? For this, I used a small cabinet hinge fastened to the clamp and a metal hose clamp that would fit over the handle of the heating tube.

I used a two-inch inside-diameter aluminum tube for the handle, which slipped over the heating tube. It didn't slip. I had to put the heat tube in a vise and hammer the larger part on. I then attached the collar and tightened it so it would be hard to turn, but it still could be rotated.

I didn't like how awkward it would be to move the hose clamp around to reset the curling iron clamp. I then realized that putting a knurled screw into the handle could tighten down to hold the hose clamp in place. This was better than needing a screwdriver to adjust the position.

I was also using the term clamp for too many items. I would soon confuse myself. Since the finished item wouldn't use a hose clamp, I decided to call it the rotator. So now I had a heating tube with a hair clamp attached by a rotator. This allowed the curling iron to be positioned and locked into place.

The next task would be to get the electrics under control. That would have to be later as I had run out of time. Dad would be picking me up soon. I updated my notebook with my progress and double-checked my sketches. I put them in a small metal toolbox along with my hairdryer parts and went to meet Dad.

I thought about buying Dad a California car as he drove us to my apartment. It might be the only way I would get mine back. I knew this wasn't a smart way to handle it but dang it. It's my car!

We hurried to clean up and change as the studio limo was due to take us to the airport. It was on time, and while the traffic was heavy, it didn't make us late. Maybe they will build a train or subway system someday to relieve the congestion. They couldn't keep building highways in LA. The city would sink from all the concrete they were pouring.

Mum's flight was on time. She was dressed to the nines, and her hair was done in a new style. It reminded me of what Grace Kelly was wearing. The only difference was her hair was jet-black. It was parted on the side with a long bob. Maybe I had been spending too much time in makeup the last few months.

She was first off the plane. She rushed to Dad and gave him a hug and a kiss. I even got a hug and a peck on the cheek. Since she was first off, and they immediately unloaded specially tagged first-class bags, we retrieved her luggage quickly and returned to the road.

She had a million questions about the house. Of course, Dad and I couldn't answer half of them. We had no idea if there was a laundry, or if there was a doorbell, or an outside clothesline, or if there was a kitchen pantry and how large it was, and did every room have closets, was the flooring the same throughout the house, and finally, were the windows single or double pane?

Dad made the smart suggestion. "Peg, instead of going straight to dinner, let's tour the house."

"Why, Jack, such a good idea," said Mum. Butter wouldn't have melted in her mouth.

I knew she could be sarcastic, but this must be a personal best.

When the limo dropped us off, we took a minute to put her bags in the house. It didn't take a genius to figure out I would be using the single bed.

Dad brought Mum up to date on tomorrow's plans.

"I know you want to see the whole house, but I should show you the sub-basement first, as we won't want to open it tomorrow."

"I will be glad to see Anna, and it will be nice to meet Nina, but it is a little inconvenient. Oh well, needs must."

The guards had been informed that Dad was buying the house, so they gave us no problems at the front gate. From the way they acted, I think they wanted to retain the business. The head guard of the three there made a point of introducing himself and giving Dad his company's brochure.

We went into the house by ourselves and immediately went to the sub-basement. Once again, we closed the door behind us. It was a good habit to get into.

Mum immediately began removing the covers from all the furniture. She thought most of it was trash, but some of it could be salvaged, like those nice Tiffany lamps. I thought they were ugly, but as long as they weren't in my room, I didn't care.

We showed Mum the stairs to the bedrooms and the escape route through the other house. She loved it.

"Secret passages are such fun. Liz and I used to roam them at Buck House. More seriously, this gives us a depth of security that I hadn't hoped for. Now, let's see your brilliant find in the safe."

I opened the safe for Mum. She reviewed everything but didn't have anything to add about the contents. However, she said she had called her friend in England and had been given some thoughts on handling things.

It now appeared Mum had a strong box at the Old Lady of Threadneedle Street. These items had been residing there all along. Not only that, but the Chancellor of the Exchequer had been notified that the contents had already been taxed in the United Kingdom, so we were free to bring the proceeds into our public finances. I guess saving a queen's life had some perks.

Mum continued, "Without these funds, we couldn't have afforded to operate this mansion. We will also have to adopt a lifestyle suitable for our residence. That means we will be mingling with a higher level of society. Jack, are you ready for this? The kids will adapt. I lived on the edge of it. You are the one who will be impacted the most."

"How different could it be?" Dad asked.

"Ask me again after you have been asked: what is your goal rating in polo?"

"My dear, I leave that to the Argentines. They seem to be good at that sort of thing."

I thought I was going to snort out of my nose at that.

"Okay, Jack, you have been warned. Good answer, though. Just make certain it isn't an Argentinian asking. They get upset at the smallest things. They have been going on about the Falklands forever."

I wondered what the Falklands were.

We locked up everything down below. Mum expressed the concern to Dad that the children would have to be told about the sub-basement and that they may innocently reveal its existence.

"Remember two Christmas ago. I took Mary shopping with me for your present. I scrimped and saved to buy you a sports coat. When you picked us up from downtown, the first thing out of Mary's mouth was, "Daddy, we bought you a sports coat.""

Dad laughed, "How can I ever forget? She had that wonderful little lisp at that time. She sprayed spit all over me when she said it. I know it spoiled your surprise, but the coat is about worn out. The story will be with us forever. Just think how you can embarrass her later."

"You're right, Jack," Mum replied slowly.

I think Mary would be paid back many times over.

Mum took a whirlwind tour of the rest of the house. She wanted an idea of what she was moving into and what work it would need. It didn't take long, as she would return for an extended tour tomorrow.

Paint, appliances, and tons of furniture were her first conclusions.

We returned to the apartment, where I graciously suggested to my parents that they take the double bed in my room. I'm not stupid.

I reread an old favorite. I thought it neat that the Boy Scouts went off-planet. It was dangerous, but any settlers on a frontier world had their lives on the line. I was rooting for Peggy but wasn't surprised when she died.

Chapter 31

Saturday, after my run, we went out for breakfast. Mum had never been to California; this was her first time getting a good look in the daylight. Her first impression was a good one. She left grey, rainy Ohio to come to sunny California. The mixture of palm trees and snowcapped mountains was a heady one.

Later, we would drive her down to the beach. After breakfast, we drove over to Monroe's. Well, Dad drove us over; this was getting to be old. I wondered what sort of car I should get him.

Anna and Nina were waiting for us. I was a little surprised when Mr. Monroe joined us. He told Mum how glad he was to meet her and that he had wondered about the Talmadge house for a long time. There were rumors of some wild parties there. There are times when you say nothing. This was one of them.

Nina brought up that it would now be Jackson House. Mum liked this idea. I think she was starting to get into this upward mobility thing. Or was it upward nobility?

Jackson House led to a discussion about letterhead and coats of arms. Dad knew his branch of the Jackson family had come to Maryland in 1635. Mum decided this was good enough; she would use the Jackson coat of arms with her viscountess crest above. She would have it made official with the College of Heralds. They may insist on a variation, but it would be based on the "Jackson" name.

I asked her what the College of Heralds was. She told me they were the official body in England that controlled such things. A coat of arms was like a trademark for a company, person, or specific family. Just because our name was Jackson didn't mean the Jackson coat of arms applied to us. That is why we would probably have a variation. She would write to the Officer in Waiting.

She finally broke down and told me she'd had an information package for years after her investiture but had done nothing about it. Now was the time.

When we arrived at the house, the ladies disappeared inside. Dad and I had seen enough. We decided to walk the grounds. We first checked out the pool house, or cabana, as the real estate agent called it.

It was nothing special. It had a wet bar, changing rooms, showers, and storage for chairs and umbrellas. There was a path going behind the fenced and gated pool area. It wasn't a high wall like the outer wall, more like to keep little kids under control. Following the path, we came to a stable that was near the back wall on the upper side of the property.

The stable was empty but in good repair. It had room for ten horses. I commented to Dad that it would be fun to have a horse. He just groaned. I think he was beginning to realize how deep he was getting.

I had to comment. "You need a truck to haul the horse trailer with your polo gear."

He smacked me up the side of the head. It hurt!

There was a gate in the rear wall. It was a serious gate. It would take a tank to batter it down. A solid wooden gate from the outside; you could see the steel reinforcing on the inside. It would take an effort to open this gate. I think it would take both Dad and me to move it. The real estate agent had explained that the land on the other side was a county park with miles of riding trails.

We continued walking around inside the walls surrounding the property. We found a large cistern sunken into the ground. It was on the property's high end so that gravity would feed the water back towards the house. A large pipe was on aqueduct legs like the Romans used coming from the house. When it rained, the runoff from the house was directed here.

The grounds further away from the house were kept in almost desert conditions. Only near the house was green grass.

After looking around, Dad commented, "Clear fields of fire."

We were getting thirsty when we walked the perimeter of the large compound. We stopped at the guardhouse to beg for a drink of water. The three guards on duty wanted to know what we thought of the place and what our plans were.

Dad told them we were going to modernize the place and live here. The senior guard, who looked like a retired LA cop, asked if we were keeping on their guard service. Dad responded that there were going to be guards. He hadn't had time to see what he would get for his money or what the competition offered.

That seemed to leave the guards uneasy, as though they knew things didn't bode well for them. I would let Mum and Dad sort it out.

Sam Monroe joined us. He'd had enough woman talk for the day. They were bent on redecorating the place, all forty-some rooms, today. So far, one good suggestion had come out: hire a decorator. Dad and Mr. Monroe talked about contractors Mr. Monroe knew in the area. He even had some thoughts on which decorators and contractors worked well together.

Dad took notes and told Mr. Monroe, "Now all I have to do, Sam, is get Peg to tell me to use these people."

Shortly thereafter, we were joined by the ladies. Mum first commented that we needed a decorator and contractor to work together.

"Good idea, Peg," replied Dad as he stuffed the notes in his pocket. This was an educational day.

We went to the Brown Derby as a group for dinner. Several people asked for my autograph, but it was nothing compared to the attention paid to Anna. She took it in stride, showing wit and patience. There could be worse role models.

I was tired, so I didn't read at all that night.

Sunday was a nothing day. Dad allowed me to drive my car! I took them on a grand tour of greater LA, ending up at the old hotel in Laguna Beach for dinner on the veranda looking out over the Pacific. Mum liked the idea of moving to California more and more.

Chapter 32

I slept well last night after Mum and Dad quieted down. They shouldn't embarrass their children like that. I was up early and performed my exercise regimen. Dick and I talked while running. I updated him on the house we were buying. He told me about another movie he had just started work on as the head stuntman. I would like to work with him someday.

Mum and Dad were both cheerful when I returned to the apartment to clean up and have breakfast. It was nice to have someone else take care of my meals. It would have been a bowl of cereal, orange juice, and coffee if it were up to me. Mum made omelets, hash browns, toast, juice, and coffee. I forgot the niceties of having a mum around. I wondered if she would make my bed.

I shouldn't have asked her.

Before I left for the studio, I received a phone call. It was the Los Angeles mayor's office. They wanted to know if I could attend a ceremony on Wednesday afternoon. It was a general presentation for those police, firemen, and other citizens who had performed a public service worthy of recognition. I gave a conditional yes, depending on the shooting schedule.

Mum had been dithering about when she would return to Ohio. Upon hearing of the ceremony, she decided to fly home on Thursday. This would allow her to attend that, plus be at the house closing on Tuesday and search for a decorator and contractor who would work together. Dad mentioned that Sam Monroe had given him several combinations that she might want to start with.

Mum took the list and started dialing Anna to get her opinion as Dad and I were leaving for the studio. I wanted to be a little early for the first day of filming *Bandits of Sherwood*. I wasn't impressed by the title, but it left no doubt about what the movie was about.

I wasn't the first to arrive, but close to it. As the cast trickled in, there was a big difference between this movie and my last. There, it was mostly twenty to thirty-year-old young men. There was enough age difference I didn't fit in.

Today, I was in the middle of the age range. Some of the littles appeared to be around eight, the oldest eighteen. About a third of them were girls. I wondered which one would be my "Maid Marian". There were several candidates.

It was none of them. Onto the set walked a tall brunette. She was gorgeous with perfectly symmetrical features. Her dark hair flowed to her waist. Her eyes were large. Her lips were a natural red. She had a body that would just not stop. In other words, she was perfect. It is a shame I disliked her immediately.

Sharon Bronson was every bit of perfection a man could ask for. I think she was twenty-two years old, but I wasn't certain. She was well-known nationally for being a total brat. She had been a child TV star who was considered a role model for all young ladies. Sharon was the font of sugar, spice, and everything nice; that changed when she was out of her parents' control.

She went wild in every way possible. The tabloids loved her. They didn't have to make up stories. She was known now as "The Bad Girl". The tabloids hoped to get titillating pictures of stars to publish. The only problem with Sharon Bronson was that her pictures were too risqué to print.

She was the talk of the makeup rooms. The studio had to bail her out of jail and tried to bury the story. Rumor had it that she was about at the end of her career. Now I understood why the producers kept putting me off when I asked who my female lead would be. They told me repeatedly it would be some name new to the business.

In my last movie, I got to meet with and even give the nod to the lady. Now, I've been blindsided. Live and learn. Mr. Baxter, my agent, my lawyers, and I would converse. In the meantime, I had to face what was coming at me.

She came directly to me. Her head didn't even come up to my chin.

Looking up, she breathed, "My, but you are a big one. This is going to be fun."

I now knew how a rabbit must feel when the snake is about ready to strike. I was paralyzed. She knew it, laughing as she strutted away. What have I gotten myself into? There was nothing I could do but ride it out.

The director and producer came in and called the group together. All the usual introductions were made. They made a big deal of how Miss Bronson had been brought in to add a little spice to what threatened to be a boring Robin Hood remake. The producer wouldn't meet my eye. I wondered what an uppercut or right cross would do to his outlook.

Those were thoughts. I took no action. This would play out one way or the other. I sincerely hoped it wouldn't turn out as Paul Grant had.

We all signed for our numbered copies of the script. We were then sent to costuming for fittings. As we finished, we would rejoin the group on the main set. I was one of the last backs. Miss Bronson had the most costumes, and they were very elaborate, so it was not surprising that she wasn't back.

The producers, directors, and writers were off the set for a meeting. There were only a few stagehands around and a whole bunch of kids. Even the parents and chaperones adjourned to the commissary for a coffee break.

It didn't take long for trouble to surface. Six of the boys, thirteen to fifteen, had squirt guns with them. They soaked each other. That was fine. They soaked me. That was okay. I wasn't thrilled, but I wouldn't melt.

What wasn't okay was when they started in on the littles. The eight and ten-year-old girls got it the worst. Several of them ended up crying.

That upset me. I did the only logical thing. I pulled them into a group in the corner. I gave everyone their marching orders. I knew where there were four fire extinguishers. These looked like giant hypodermics. They were brass, weighed about ten pounds each, and held a gallon of water. They worked with a plunger.

I positioned the girls at a fire hose. I turned the wheel so it was loose enough that they could operate it. We uncoiled it, and six small girls held the hose ready while one was to turn it on when the boys ran into the trap. Three of the littlest boys and I took the fire extinguishers and drove the big boys right towards the girls.

Those fire extinguishers could put out the water. We were drowning the older boys. They ran right where I wanted them.

At my shout of "Now!" the girls turned on the fire hose. It was all they could do to hold the hose down on the boys, but they managed. There was enough pressure the boys were knocked from their feet. Talk about soaked!

I hurried over and closed the fire hose valve. My gang of little's were doing a victory dance. Even the boys who had been knocked over were laughing.

My plan was perfect except for one small detail. When a fire hose was turned on, it caused the system pressure to drop, which in turn set off a fire alarm. We had the studio fire department and police within ten minutes at our site.

To say the firemen were upset was putting it mildly. At least they called and turned back the Burbank Fire Department before they arrived. The Burbank police did show up.

Of course, with all this commotion, the parents who left their little angels all came running in. The producer, director, and writers weren't far behind. As a matter of fact, within minutes, half the studio was present. Production had been halted on other sets until things were settled.

I could see that this wasn't going to be pretty, so I stepped up to the fire chief, who Mr. Monroe had joined. I explained that the getting out of hand was my fault. You could tell Mr. Monroe wasn't thrilled.

"Rick, as soon as I knew it was this set, I thought you would be at the bottom. Well, we now have lemons. Let's make lemonade."

He then proceeded to show why he was the president of Warner Brothers. He gathered the parents together and announced.

"This impromptu play gives us a huge publicity opportunity. There is enough blame to go around, so let's not even go there. These were bored kids on the set, letting off a little steam and coming together. The only problem is we don't have any footage, so we are going to do it again for the cameras.

Everyone hustled, and the set was dried out. Clothes changed to movie costumes, and the fire extinguishers were reloaded. By this time, Sharon Bronson was back on set, so there was a revision to the original plan. She and I were now the ones who quickly made the plan after the older boys soaked the littles.

She was the one who turned on the fire hose while the little girls held it down. That part went better as one more person was on the hose. It was filmed perfectly but was done as though it was picked up impromptu rather than staged. Of course, they had to bring the fire engines with lights and sirens back onto the set as if they were just arriving.

It wasn't as much fun as the first time. Especially when Mr. Monroe had a couple of stagehands bring in an empty water trough. He had it put down in a corner.

"Once more, Rick, and I will rewrite the movie so you live in it."

He wasn't a happy man. He did ruin the effect a little when he picked up one of the fire extinguishers and gave it a big squirt.

"These would be fun at our pool if they weren't heavy."

Hmm, you could make them out of plastic. They would be super-squirt guns. I would have to talk to my engineers in Columbus.

One thing noticeable was that the kids were all laughing and joking around. The little girls would break out in a victory dance around the older teenage boys. The boys took it. If nothing else, the cast was bonding.

As he left, Mr. Monroe, seeing the same bonding, said, "Worse things have happened. You got lucky, Rick, but please keep it down to a dull roar."

Now, what have I ever done to cause excitement?

The biggest surprise was Sharon Bronson. She stood beside me and said, "That is the most fun I have ever had on a set, and I didn't even get in on the original water fight."

"Events did get out of hand," I confessed.

"It was a lot more fun than the parties I always attend. All they do is drink, smoke, brag, and try to have sex with me."

"Tough life," I replied.

"It is getting to be. I'm close to losing my career. My parents won't speak to me, my agent and business manager is a thief, and the only people who will go out with me are low-life scum.

"I know it's my fault. I wanted to demonstrate I was grown up and ready for adult parts. So, I tried to live like an adult. Unfortunately, the people I chose to live it with were the wrong ones."

"What are you going to do?"

"I have no idea. I'm caught in a vicious circle and can't see a way out."

I thought of something, then stopped and thought some more. If this worked, it would be great. If it backfired, it would hurt a lot of people.

"May I call you Sharon?" I asked.

"Yes, if I can call you Rick."

"Sharon, I know some people who could help you, but you would have to share what you have just told me and then be ready to do what they tell you."

"As long as I don't end up in jail, I will do about anything. My money is almost gone, and the studio has me on warning."

"Can you join me and my parents for dinner along with someone else if they can make it?"

"Yes, I can. If I didn't join you, I would be drinking at some dive."

"Excuse me for a minute while I make a phone call."

The day was shot as far as the film was concerned, which wasn't good because of the tight schedule, so I could go to the studio office for a call. Mum, Dad, Miss Romanov, Mr. Monroe, and I were having dinner at the Brown Derby. Nina was off on a class trip to San Francisco.

I called my parents and gave a quick explanation that I wanted to bring Sharon Bronson to dinner and that she needed some help.

Mum wasn't thrilled; she'd kept up with Miss Bronson's exploits more than I had. I explained that she was reaching out for help and that I didn't want to turn her away. Mum did note that she was an accomplished actress, so it may not be what I think.

She told me she would call Miss Romanov and Mr. Monroe, inviting them but allowing them to beg off.

They didn't. At six o'clock, we met at the Brown Derby. Sharon had dressed in what I suspected were her most conservative clothes. Mr. Cobb still looked like he wanted to turn her away.

Miss Romanov made eyes at him, and he relented immediately. If she looked at me that way, I would also relent. From the look on Dad's face, he would, too, and from the look on Mum's face, Dad had some questions to answer.

Other than that, we made nice. Someone, probably Mr. Monroe, requested a private dining room. When we had all eaten, I looked at Sharon and said, "The ball is now in your court."

I must give her credit. She told it all unemotionally, not trying to shift blame, sticking to the facts.

She ended, "Today, it all came to a head. I acted like a kid for a few minutes and then realized how much fun I used to have. I would like to get back to my old life, not childish parts or being a kid, but be someone who people look up to and respect for what I have done. I know I'm about out of rope, and now Rick has thrown me a lifeline."

There wasn't a dry eye in the room. Mum and Anna swept Sharon up and away to the lady's room. Dad, Mr. Monroe, and I exchanged looks.

Mr. Monroe told Dad, "If we can ever get this boy to quit being a hero, he might amount to something."

"Sam, when you figure that out, let me know."

Mr. Monroe told us, "I can help with the combined agent-business manager problem. I will have a couple of studio lawyers at her agent's office tomorrow. They will demand to see her financial records. That way, he will be on the hook for whatever money remains. He will notify her when they leave he is no longer her agent."

"Why would he do that?" Dad asked.

"They are going to imply that she is being kicked off the movie because of today. The news will still be garbled about what went on, so he will buy that it is her fault. As long as she brings in money, she would have to prove misconduct by him to break her contract. He will drop her as soon as he thinks she is no longer a golden goose."

I asked, "What will she do for an agent in the meantime?"

"You are going to spend some of your credit with John Baxter and ask him to act as her agent and business manager until she can line someone else up."

The ladies returned to the table, and Mr. Monroe explained what he planned to do on the agent front.

Miss Romanov said, "Peg and I are going to work with Susan Wallace to remake Sharon's image. Rick, we will probably have some exclusives for your friends in the newspapers.

Sharon, whose face had that just-washed look from crying your eyes out, asked apprehensively, "What papers?"

"The *LA Examiner, Variety,* and the tabloid with the largest national circulation," I told her.

Miss Romanov added, "Sharon will be staying at my house for a while. She needs the support and none of the temptations. I almost went her route, so I know how hard it can be. Tomorrow evening, Peg, Sharon, and I will have a planning session, and then we will go shopping."

Dad and Mr. Monroe just nodded their heads in agreement. I had nothing to add.

We all agreed that the great water fight, as it was becoming known, would be left as a confused story until Sharon was free of that agent. It was a good thing we had a plan. When we got back to the apartment, the phone was ringing. Dad unplugged it from the wall, and we said good night. I drifted right off. I have no idea what Mum and Dad did.

Chapter 33

Tuesday morning started normally and stayed that way until I got to the studio. Bill the gate guard had a note for me. It was a reminder from Mr. Monroe to call Mr. Baxter. Sharon Bronson made it through the night without causing anyone to change their minds about her need for help.

I stopped at the office and made my phone call.

When I asked Mr. Baxter for a favor, he replied, "Certainly."

When I told him what it was, all I heard was dead silence.

I finally asked, "Are you still there?"

"Yes, I am Rick. I'm in shock that of all the things you could ask of me, I wouldn't have dreamed of this. I owe you so that I will help, but God help us all if it goes sour."

"Thanks, Mr. Baxter."

After his commitment, I related the entire story to him. He was still hesitant, but when he heard that Mr. Monroe, Miss Romanov, and my parents were all coming together to help, he was more positive.

"Keep me posted, Rick, so I know when and where to contact her."

"She will contact you and ask you for your help. She is the beggar here."

"You certainly show love in a tough way, Rick,"

"Sometimes, that is all you can do. This isn't love. It's just human kindness."

"Whatever you want to call it, you're a good man."

After ending our call, I went to the set. This was the walk-through day. We had our scripts. Now we were walking through the basic storyline. *Bandits* purported to be the story of young Robin Locksley and how he became Robin Hood. Forget that part about him coming back from the Crusades and seeing injustice.

Our storyline was that he started as a teenager and grew into the role of defender of the weak. It starts with expert archer Robin being cheated out of the county archery prize by the future Sheriff of Nottingham. The future sheriff, who we quickly started calling Junior on set, was competing against Robin in the tournament. The current sheriff and father of Junior became Senior.

Robin, a sixteen-year-old lad, put three arrows in the bullseye. Junior had two in the center and one in the outer ring. However, when they brought the targets to Senior who was the judge, Junior's target had been switched. Now not only were Junior's all in the center of the bullseye, but the next two also split the center arrow.

Junior was awarded the Loving Cup trophy for his fantastic shooting. Robin was given a copper penny for his efforts.

Of course, now, Robin was honor-bound to steal the cup from Junior, which he did. In turn, Junior had to steal it back from Robin. These thefts continued throughout the story. Each time the cup gets a ding or two. By the movie's end, the cup is a battered wreck having pride of place in...well, pay to see the movie.

Of course, there is a love interest as Robin meets Maid Marian. As normal for Hollywood, the first meeting is a disaster as they take an instant dislike to each other. Love blossoms as events transpire, and they are thrown together and forced to work as a team.

It has its funny moments, well, a lot of funny moments. Like when Little John and Robin are fighting with quarterstaffs over who has the right-of-way over a footbridge.

They are going at it hot and heavy until a little old nun comes along and shoves them both into the water so that she can use the bridge. Not a high-brow movie. The target audience is teenagers. They will love it.

Things turn serious when Senior raises the tax rate so high the villagers will starve if they pay it. The tax collector, accompanied by a small army, takes the money from the village.

Of course, Robin gets in on it. He makes sure they get a paid-in-full receipt from the tax collector. Then the men of the village are forced to work under the supervision of half the tax collector's troops to repair a bridge that Robin undermined.

With the villagers' alibi in place, Robin leads the children of the village to seize the funds back.

They are successful. Boy wins girl, and legend is born. It sounded hokey as all get out, but it would appeal to the American teenage sense of fun and justice if done right. If that happened, the backers, me included, would make money, appealing to our sense of fun and justice, and the heck with the critics.

One thing very noticeable was that while the set was full of kids, they were paying attention and not bickering or goofing off. Larger kids were holding small kids up, so they were able to see. I hadn't seen this much teamwork among the actors until the last weeks of *Sir Nick*.

After our basic introduction to the story, we were given a quick tour of the sets that had been built. This would never be known as a big-budget movie. We had an English village already at the studio at the time. It consisted of the interiors of two peasant huts and six false-front houses. Our castle had four interior rooms, a false front, and a large courtyard.

Any outdoor shots would be done in the open fields or woods on the backlot. I didn't bother to look them up, but I bet the trees in our woods wouldn't be found in Sherwood Forest.

When the tour was completed, I reported to make-up, and just like that, the filming process started. We broke for lunch at one o'clock. A group of us guys wandered over to the commissary. I had all the boys. The girls accompanied Sharon Bronson.

If we had two gangs developing, I would bet on the girls winning any gang war. It didn't come to that. The boys were doing the usual stupid things teenage boys do. Our littles, boys under ten, were trying to emulate the older boys. I wasn't sure it would end well.

I watched the girls and realized the older girls were watching the boys, like a rancher checking the herd for the best stock. The little girls were watching the older girls check out the boys. I'm not sure that would end well from the whispers and giggles.

Mr. Monroe walked over to Sharon and said something to her. They stepped aside, but she waved me over to join them. "Rick, you were in at the beginning of this. I would like you to hear what has happened."

Mr. Monroe eyed Sharon and asked, "Are you certain you want Rick here? This involves your finances and job situation."

"Yes, I'm certain. Rick is the one who brought the people together who are trying to help me; I think he deserves to know."

"Okay then, it is all good news. This morning a lawyer showed up at your ex-agent's office."

The word ex-agent was enough to get a big smile from Sharon.

"He handed you a formal letter from the studio, demanding a ten-million-dollar performance bond be posted. Warner Brothers has grave concerns over your conduct and its impact on the movie. As your business agent, we demanded that he immediately write a one hundred thousand dollar check to cover this bond.

"He refused, stating that he was no longer your agent. Our lawyer demanded that it be put in writing immediately so we could pursue you. Your now ex-agent did it at once. That lawyer left and met across the street with another group. The district attorney and several policemen were waiting for this event. They served a subpoena on the bum for fraud.

"The subpoena was for your financial records. It turned out the guy was a poor thief. He transferred your money to his accounts. He wasn't even smart enough to move the money to hidden accounts. Those accounts are now frozen.

"He had taken almost everything you had, three million dollars. It is estimated that you have completely lost a quarter million, but all things considered, you have come out alright. The creep was hauled out in handcuffs.

"He left two hundred thousand in your account, so your immediate financial needs are taken care of."

Sharon replied, "This is better news than I ever dreamed of. Unfortunately, I have to find another agent."

"That's taken care of, Sharon," I interrupted. "John Baxter has agreed to handle you until you can get settled."

I received a quick hug for that. For a female whom I disliked yesterday, she sure felt good in a hug.

Mr. Monroe continued. "Anna Romanov and I would like to meet with you later today. We would like to teach you how to assemble a financial team with checks and balances."

Sharon gushed, "Anna is fabulous. I spent last night at her house. I wouldn't have gotten through the night sober without her. She has asked me to stay with her until things are settled. I'm going shopping with her and Rick's Mum tonight. My wardrobe is going to be completely changed to that of the person I want to be."

After all this good news, we returned to work and continued until six o'clock. I met with Coach Palmer and told him the movie demands were such that I probably couldn't continue my daily lessons. He thought for a moment and asked me, "How serious are you?"

"Very, I need to learn this."

"Would you mind working weekends for the next month?"

"I can do that."

"Rick, you are paying me well for this, and it turns out I need the money, so I'm willing to work if you are."

We shook hands and agreed to put in eight hours on Saturdays and four hours on Sundays for the next month.

Dad picked me up in my T-Bird. How was I ever going to get my car back? He told me they had closed on Jackson House earlier in the day. He and Mum had spent the afternoon talking to her first pick for a decorator, and then the decorator recommended the contractor. Mum liked the decorator and his ideas. Dad liked the contractor.

Dad commented, "At least he is a man."

It would be interesting to meet Sergio, Mum's decorator.

Mum gave Sergio his first assignment, to have a brass plaque made for the pillar at the front gate. It would say Jackson House. Dad had been busy walking the contractor through the house and showing what had to be done to bring the house into shape. He hoped to have a signed agreement in place with the front money by tomorrow.

He also toured a couple of buildings in Los Angeles as possible office space. One building caught his interest. It was on the edge of an area that was being rebuilt. Like many neighborhoods, it had started on the high end and then gone downhill for the next fifty years.

Now, the buildings were cheap enough that they were being bought and updated. The decline in pricing would turn around, and those who bought in early would make a nice profit.

"Dad, are you thinking of buying the whole building?"

"It would make sense to be our own landlord."

"What about the other buildings in the block?"

"There are two others between us and the area that have already been redone."

"Why didn't you choose the one near the good area?"

"It has limited parking. That is a problem with the whole block. Less so with the one I picked."

"Is there any place nearby that could be made into a parking lot?"

"There is a vacant lot across the street. Bums use it now. The city owns it and won't develop it until the buildings are redone. No one wants to renovate the buildings until there is parking. It is a circular problem. No one will go first, so nothing moves."

"Dad, who are we seeing tomorrow at lunch?"

"The mayor of Los Angeles," Dad slowly replied.

"Why don't you explain to him that you want to update one of those buildings and that you will go first if he guarantees the parking?"

"No, Rick, we will go first on all three buildings. All the buildings will be worth a bundle if the parking is there. We can buy all three and then upgrade one at a time. The first one will finance the renovation of the second. The second will finance the third. One thing I have learned is how leverage works in real estate."

"Will it hurt our capital position and cash flow?"

I learned a few things from my reading on economics. It was still hit or miss, but I felt more comfortable than I did several months ago.

"It shouldn't. Buying and renovating the three buildings will take an initial one hundred and fifty thousand. We received your first-quarter checks on the adjustable showerhead to offset that. Considering it was not a full quarter, it went very well. The checks from all the companies totaled ninety thousand dollars."

This was wonderful news. We had hoped to make fifty thousand a quarter from the showerheads. It also didn't include any income from Detroit Faucet. That money was being put right back into the company. Mark and I agreed that he would take a salary and that we would reinvest everything for the first year to give the company a solid start.

This made me look forward to the second-quarter results. Furthermore, the hairdryer will be on the market during the second quarter. Dad had a busy day. He told me we were on our own for dinner. The ladies had gone shopping and would eat out, the ladies being Mum, Anna, and Sharon. They would probably eat a salad somewhere.

He also told me that Susan Wallace had signed on and that the ladies would meet on Wednesday morning to discuss handling Sharon's changes publicly.

Dad and I chose In-N-Out. We went back to the apartment and watched *Dragnet*, followed by the *Eddie Fisher Show* (Dad's choice) and then the *George Burns Show*. When Mum got home, I told Dad about my dinner with Mr. Burns and his wife Gracie.

She was looking a little frazzled. That meant she had one hair out of place.

Dad picked up on it immediately, "What's wrong, Peg?"

"We ran into some of Sharon's old friends. They wanted her to join them, actually join them, and pay for everything in a drinking party. She told them no. They were insistent and tried to grab her. Anna and I put a stop to it."

"And how did you do that?" Dad asked quietly.

I think he was scared of the answer.

"We didn't shoot them if that is what you are asking. We just waved our pistols in front of them. They decided they needed to be somewhere else."

"No harm done then," said Dad.

Mum was unwinding from her tense look as she talked.

"You should have seen the revolver Anna pulled out of her purse. It was a gold plated .38 with pearl handles."

"Wherever did she get something like that?" inquired Dad.

"I also wondered. She was given it by a friend, who was a lady detective in Australia in the 1920s. The detective is retired now and passed it on to Anna. She thought that as a movie star, Anna might need it."

Mum had her usual Walther PPK with her. She had always carried a pistol in her purse, and we kids had been taught to respect it and also how to use it. One thing I had never asked her was why she chose that weapon. I did now.

She replied, "James convinced me after his Beretta jammed on a mission."

She bursts out laughing, "You should have seen the look on your face. There is no bloody James Bond; he is Ian Fleming's fictional creature. I switched to the PPK after my Beretta jammed. All the agents changed over at the same time. Fleming heard about it and wrote it into his story."

Someday, I would corner Mum and get her full story, but not today.

"Is Sharon okay?"

"Oh yes, she now wants to get herself a weapon. Anna is going to enroll her in a gun safety and shooting class. Sharon wants a gold-plated pistol just like Anna's.

"Would you like one?" Dad inquired.

"Jack, they are just a tool, not an ornament," she replied.

Her reply was not very convincing. I wondered how one went about buying a gold-plated PPK. It must be new because we would never get hers away from her long enough to have it plated.

Dad and I exchanged a quick look. I think great minds and all that.

I had too much on my mind to read that night. Thinking about Sharon reminded me of that book where the white man's burden was discussed. The author was writing about the United States in the Philippines, but Sharon qualified as my burden. Heck, I didn't even particularly like her. Now she was my problem.

Then there was Jackson House, the new offices, staffing for the offices, plus an electric curling iron to build. I started chuckling as I thought of the great squirt-gun fight at the studio. I dodged much trouble with that one, but it was funny. I wish I had a large squirt gun like that to take to Bellefontaine High.

I thought about that and realized I could have a giant squirt gun even though I might not take it to Bellefontaine High. I scribbled some notes on the pad near my bed and finally went to sleep.

Chapter 34

On Tuesday morning, I called Paul Samson, the mechanical engineer I worked with in Columbus on the hairdryer project.

After getting past his surprise at hearing from me, I went, "Paul, I have an idea for a toy."

"What's that, Ricky?"

The use of Ricky bothered me a little. I was so used to being called Rick as a sign of my growing up. However, in fairness, he wasn't there to see it. I would probably be Ricky to some people all my life.

I described my idea of a giant-sized squirt gun.

"Ricky, it will hold a lot of water but won't shoot any further than a regular squirt gun."

"This is the clever part. We will increase the water pressure by having a pump like a bicycle tire pump. Instead of the long cylinder they have, we will pump up the air pressure inside the body of the squirt gun."

"I get it, Rick. A regular squirt gun pumps up the pressure with its trigger. This way, the trigger would just open the outlet to let the water go. If you held the trigger back, you would have water flow for as long as you had pressure. The water shoots out as far as the pressure would push it."

"You have got it, Paul. Get together with Don Thompson and come up with some designs that look like space guns. I don't want any that look like a real pistol or rifle. That could cause problems."

"Yeah, I could see the headlines now. A kid holds up a bank with a squirt gun. Banker drowns, prosecutor asking for the death penalty."

"Well, maybe not that far out, but you get my meaning."

"How far do you want us to go on this?"

"Come up with several designs and get quotes on the plastic prototype tooling.

"Come to think of it. I want one special mold made only for me, a Colt .45 six-shooter that can be painted to look real. I owe Mr. Wayne a soaking or two."

"It's your life."

After the phone call, I did my morning exercises and ran. I tried to ignore the noises coming from my bedroom.

Dick Wyman was at the track as usual, and we joined up. He wanted to know all about the happenings at the studio. The rumor mill was going wild about Sharon Bronson, me, the studio fire department, the police, Bronson's agent being hauled off in handcuffs, and finally, guns being waved in one of the fanciest dress shops in town. What gives?

Wow, putting it that way, it got a little wild. I brought him up to date on events. He was a little dubious about Sharon wanting to reform but would withhold judgment. He did acknowledge that with Anna and Mum handling her, she would be on a short leash.

As we ran, I had an idea. I didn't want to go too quickly, but I did ask Dick if he and Janice still wanted to move into a house. They did even if they had to rent one. The apartment was getting cramped, and they were thinking of starting a family. He wanted to know why I asked. I told him I had heard something but wanted to check it out before saying anything.

I could check it out at breakfast.

"Mum and Dad, have you given any thought as to what you will be doing with the house outside of the wall?"

They hadn't.

"I was thinking we can't let it sit empty, but we would have to have someone we trusted implicitly in it. I was thinking of us letting Dick and Janice Wyman live there rent-free. They have done so much for me, at least kept me out of trouble. It would pay them back, and I would trust them with our secret exit."

Mum and Dad exchanged glances.

Mum replied, "That is not a bad idea, Rick. I will have a background check run on them. If they don't have any problems, we will make the offer. We will tell them of the exit only after they have accepted the offer."

I went into the studio. It was serious work with no messing around. This movie was on a very tight budget, and they couldn't afford any overruns. Like most movies, they were renting the sets, crew, and equipment from Warner Brothers. A day too long in making the movie might break the budget. A week would destroy it. Goofing off wasn't budgeted.

That is not to mean that anyone was unpleasant. It was just the opposite. If anyone got a little out of sorts and threatened to slow things down, someone would pull a squirt gun out of a hiding spot and pretend to shoot them. I never knew you could hide squirt guns in so many places.

It did bother me a little when Friar Tuck pulled one out of his Bible. He had to show me it was not a real Bible. It was a small cigar box that was painted black with gold leaf lettering.

At noon, I had permission to leave and go downtown for the mayor's presentation. My parents and I met at the studio. We were joined by Mr. Monroe, Miss Wallace, and Mr. Baxter. We used a studio limo. They were certainly handy. Maybe we should buy one.

At City Hall, the mayor and a ton of reporters were waiting. The day wasn't just about me; it was very little about me. This was a ceremony they held biannually to honor the firemen, policemen, and anyone else who had done something noteworthy for the city. They took care of the police and firemen first. There were only two civilians, me and a guy who had pulled a kid out of a burning building before the firemen got there.

The other guy was first; he received the Mayor's Medal of Honor for saving a life. I was presented the same award for preventing the loss of life, in this case convincing the bank robbers to give up without the police having to charge into real danger. The mayor gave a short speech and shook my hand after hanging the medal around my neck.

Since I was the last one, we chatted briefly. I introduced my dad, who was right there. I backed away as Dad switched into business mode. A policeman who turned out to be the chief of police came over and shook my hand.

"I was on wave three at Omaha Beach. I know what you saved my boys from."

I heard machine-gun fire rattling off a landing craft door for a moment and knew I was not a hero.

"Sir, you are the hero. All I did was shoot some arrows from safety. I am glad it closed the situation down, but I have no illusions about my heroism."

"Why do you say that, Rick?" he asked.

I told him about Bill Samson, who was on wave two.

"You do understand then."

He handed me a leather wallet. "Don't overuse this, but we still owe you one."

He walked away. I opened the wallet. Inside was a shield from the Los Angeles Police Department. There was an identification card with my picture and information. It was headed Honorary Member.

"Wow," was all I could say.

I was getting a badge collection.

I resolved never to use it unless it was dire. I knew it would get me out of a speeding ticket, but that wasn't my style, or at least I hoped it wasn't. I would keep it in the glove box of the T-Bird. That is if I could get my car back from Dad.

Dad was done talking to the mayor and now was exchanging cards with one of the mayor's aides. Their talks went fine. I didn't get a chance to ask him as I got cornered by several reporters. Susan Wallace was right there to bail me out.

Fortunately, I didn't need help. They asked the questions Sharon had predicted, and I gave them the answers she had helped me develop. They were her thoughts, in my words.

"Yes, it felt good to help the police. Yes, I could pull that bow; no, I wouldn't want to always shoot people."

Where do they learn to ask such stupid questions?

When it got to the great squirt-gun fight, I told it like it was, except I neglected to clarify that Sharon Bronson wasn't in the first round. It made it look like we had teamed up, me leading the young boys and she the little girls to save them all from those big bad teenagers. Except the teenagers weren't bad; we all had a blast!

They wanted to know about Sharon and her agent. I could say that I wasn't there, so I didn't know what was happening. They should call the DA's office.

Someone asked if it was true that Sharon and I were dating.

The answer was "No."

The next was about the gunfight at the OK corral. Well, the ladies showing their shooting irons to the guys trying to hassle Sharon. I was told that Anna Romanov had been identified as one of the women. Did I know the other? I looked over at Sharon. She nodded yes.

"Yes, I know the other woman. It was Viscountess Jackson."

That set off a small firestorm of questions. Nobility was involved. They wanted to know more about the viscountess.

I shrugged and turned to Mum. "You want to handle these?"

"Certainly, dear," Mum replied as she turned to the press.

"Sharon Bronson is a personal friend with whom I was shopping. We were approached by thugs who wouldn't take no for an answer, so we became more emphatic in our no.

"Who are you?" one intrepid reporter asked.

"Why, I am Viscountess Jackson, Rick's Mum. I'm so sorry, but our time is up."

We tried to get out but were blocked by the mayor's entourage. Being the good politician that he was, he couldn't miss a photo op with Mum. He was gracious enough to allow Dad and me into the picture. He came across as a decent guy.

From the body language earlier, I think Dad got some sort of a deal on the parking lot. Dad confirmed it on the way back to the studio. If he bought the buildings, they would convert the vacant lot into a parking lot. He was also invited to a fund-raiser for the mayor's reelection campaign. It was the sort of offer you couldn't refuse.

He could be listed as a co-host for the event for one hundred dollars. He didn't even have to attend or send money. Dad elected to mail a check.

I got back to the studio several hours later. There was still time for some lighting checks that had to be done for each scene. It was seven o'clock before I got out. Dad had been waiting for a while, but he didn't seem to mind. He told me that just sitting in the warm California air on an April night was wonderful. It was raining earlier in Ohio when he and Mum called home to talk to my sister and brothers.

Mum fixed us a really good meatloaf dinner. It was the first truly home-cooked meal I had in months. After dinner, Dad and I got our marching orders from Mum about what must be done with Jackson House. She left Dad with a long list of follow-up items.

As far as the timing on all of this went, they would let the kids finish the school year in Bellefontaine. They would move as early as possible in the summer, remembering that we were going to visit Mum's mother in August. Dad was to push the contractor.

He also had to take care of the renovations in the sub-basement on his own. There was no rush on that as long as there was a telephone, food, and water. Mum would be making periodic trips out to work with the decorator. Furnishing a forty-plus room house was a large job.

Besides the above, Dad had his lists of things to do on the office buildings. The first, of course, was buying them, subcontracting the work, and then renting them out.

Then, I added my thoughts as to what staffing we needed for the business.

When you got down to it, there was a need for basic business functions. There had to be accounting, human resources, an insurance specialist, and someone who would handle purchasing, probably HR since there would only be office supplies.

Then, there were the true core people needed. I needed someone to market licenses on a worldwide basis. We would have to have a patent attorney on retainer. Engineers would have to be available to turn any idea in crude prototype form into reality.

Then, a firm to keep track of my investments and update them as needed. Dad's job as my business manager was to line up all this support. I expressed that to him, and he reminded me he had one more item in his job jar.

I asked what it was.

"To slap you upside your head when you get too big for your britches."

I started to bristle at that but then settled down. He was right. I needed someone who could do that. There were too many unknowns; I needed all the help. Dad was going to be one busy man. He even joked to Mum that maybe we should help me get emancipated, and then I would have to do all this. Mum was not amused.

After our busy day, we all retired early. I didn't feel like reading.

Chapter 35

Dad and I saw Mum down to the limo in the morning, taking her to the airport. After hugs, kisses, and the usual admonitions, I did my run. Afterward, Dad dropped me off at the studio.

Insult to injury, Dad told me he would attach one of those knobs to the steering wheel to help turn corners. At least he gave me my bedroom back. I would rather have had the car.

Thursday was a full-blown day of filming at the studio. It was the hardest day I had ever put in on a movie. It worked without letting up. The only break I had all day was at lunch. At the commissary, I looked around, and a few people were dressed strangely. I even mentioned that to a couple of office guys sitting there.

They glanced at each other, and one said, "Right, Robin Hood."

Oops.

Dad picked me up at six, and we did the In-N-Out thing again. Susan Wallace joined us. She showed us copies of the stories about the mayor's presentation. They were all favorable. Then, she gave us copies of their writing about Sharon Bronson.

The stories were all over the map. Some had it right, the bad girl trying to turn good. Others had a leopard that wouldn't change its spots. The one that had me laughing was where she was having my child. Where do they get this stuff?

The stories about Sharon trying to change her image were all from my friends in the media. Sharon talked to them for me. She had made the calls but had several quotes from me to fill out their stories. Susan told me that in all her time with Paul Grant, he had never developed media contacts like mine.

At the apartment, I typed up my notes about the electric curling iron and made sketches of what I thought the switches and the heating element would look like.

I also told Dad about the super squirt gun I was having made. He got into that; I thought his idea of a canteen with a hose to the squirt gun would work. Having a backpack with a large water bottle was over the top.

No kid would want to lug around a backpack.

After that, I fell asleep watching TV, so Dad woke me and sent me to bed. No comment. I had a good night's sleep.

Friday was more of the same. We didn't finish until after eight o'clock. The union guys loved the overtime, the rest of us not so much. The littles were sleeping in a corner. The set dresser put a canvas drop cloth in a corner. We had a pile of little kids sleeping there. They were cute.

Finally, we were all released. The director approached me and, to my surprise, thanked me.

"Rick, you kept with it all day. That is appreciated; we are under a financial gun here, so your work ethic is a real plus."

I think it was the first time that I realized I was the star of the film and would set the tone for the whole movie. I had to be on my toes.

Thank goodness we had Saturday off. Dad dropped me at the studio, where I went to work with Coach Palmer. He wasn't finding it as easy to toss me around these days. The highlight of the day for me was the first time he had to slap the mat in surrender.

We had to take several breaks throughout the day. I went over to the prop shop and worked on the heating elements. It only took a simple winding and an off-on switch. The next issue to be addressed was how much heat.

I found an old Variac transformer in the shop so that the current could be changed as needed; this, in turn, changed the heat output. I created a chart and found a thermocouple along with a sensor. Now, the heat could be varied and measured. This is what I would ask makeup to try.

There had to be enough heat to set the hair, but not so much that it set it on fire or melted it. I thought it would be between two to three hundred degrees Fahrenheit. Putting the contraption on a wheeled cart, it was ready to go on Monday morning.

Sunday was half a day practicing hand-to-hand. Dad came along and watched. He and Coach Palmer got along well. Dad told Coach that we were moving out here and asked if he would be interested in giving private lessons to my sister and brothers. The boys, I could understand, but Mary was so young. Dad set me straight about a young lady having to be able to defend herself. She might not always have a big brother around to defend her.

Well, there was no question that I and my brothers would look out for her. I just hoped it never got that serious because I would kill for her if I had to. Anyway, Coach said he would be glad to give private lessons.

Dad and I spent the rest of the day cruising around Hollywood, learning our way around the area. It would have been a wonderful afternoon if he had let me drive.

Finished for now

Back Matter

To be continued in Book 5: Star to Deckhand: The Richard Jackson Saga[1]

enelsonauthor.com[2]

For information on hiring Janet E. Rupert to edit your fiction project, email:

janeteditorrupert@gmail.com

-

---

1. https://d.docs.live.net/f59a06b92f374959/Desktop/Jackson%20Stories/eBooks/
   5.%09https://www.amazon.com/gp/product/B07XCQ834J
2.   **https://enelsonauthor.com/**

Other books by Ed Nelson

The Richard Jackson Saga
Book 1 The Beginning
Book 2 Schooldays
Book 3 Hollywood
Book 4 In the Movies
Book 5 Star to Deckhand
Book 6 Surfing Dude
Book 7 Third Time is a Charm
Book 8 Oxford University
Book 9 Cold War
Book 10 Taking Care of Business
Book 11 Interesting Times
Book 12 Escape from Siberia
Book 13 Regicide
Book 14 What's Under, Down Under?
Book 15 The Lunar Kingdom
Book 16 First Steps
In the Richard Jackson World
Mary, Mary
Stand-Alone Story
Ever and Always
Cast in Time Series
Book 1: Baron
Book 2: Baron of the Middle Counties
Book 3: Count
Book 4: Earl
Book 5: Earl of the Marches

Did you love *In the Movies*? Then you should read *Star to Deckhand* by Ed Nelson!

Star to Deckhand has Rick working and living in California. Starring in a new movie has its challenges, whilst going on holiday is a world of its own. As Rick gains skills in his new role as an actor he finds that he can sing, to a point. A dark and dangerous side of the family comes forth when Soviet Agents kidnap his sister. The move into Jackson House has its surprises. While the family flies to England for their holiday, Rick works his way there as a deckhand on a freighter. Cuba, Argentina, Africa, and England each have their own adventures for our maturing young man. This tongue in cheek saga is all true, give or take a lie or two.